Tony Parsons, OAM, is a bestselling writer of rural Australian novels. He is the author of *The Call of the High Country*, *Return to the High Country*, *Valley of the White Gold*, *Silver in the Sun* and *Back to the Pilliga*. Tony has worked as a sheep and wool classer, journalist, news editor, rural commentator, consultant to major agricultural companies and an award-winning breeder of animals and poultry. He also established 'Karrawarra', one of the top kelpie studs in Australia, and was awarded the Order of Australia Medal for his contribution to the propagation of the Australian kelpie. Tony lives with his wife near Toowoomba and maintains a keen interest in kelpie breeding.

TONY PARSONS

Return to Moondilla

ARENA
ALLEN&UNWIN

Arena Books, an imprint of
Allen & Unwin
83 Alexander Street
Crows Nest NSW 2065
Australia
Phone:(61 2) 8425 0100
Email: info@allenandunwin.com
Web: www.allenandunwin.com

Cataloguing-in-Publication details are available
from the National Library of Australia
www.trove.nla.gov.au

ISBN 978 1 76011 146 5

Internal design by Bookhouse
Set in 11.75/18.75 pt Sabon LT Pro by Bookhouse, Sydney
Printed and bound in China by Hang Tai Printing Company Limited

10 9 8 7 6 5 4

Dedicated to my daughter Holly Lorraine Parsons,
who tragically died in a car crash on 23rd August 2014.
Holly touched everyone who knew her.
She would have loved the Chief of this story.
Her two German Shepherds, Dougal and Wishes,
were with her and both survived the crash.

PROLOGUE

The white half-cabin launch rocked gently in the ocean's swell, very close to the river's mouth. There was a fitful north-easterly breeze. A breeze was always coming in off the ocean—only its direction changed.

Sam Corrigan and his son, Bevan, were fishing the run-in tide. They'd caught three flathead and hoped to catch a couple more before they pulled up anchor and headed back to shore. Some of Moondilla's lights still glowed in the half-dawn, and away to the west the line of the Range was just coming into view.

'Ready for a cuppa and a sandwich?' Sam asked his son.

'More than ready, Dad. I could eat a horse and chase the rider.'

Sam grinned. Bevan was eighteen, a champion swimmer, and his pride and joy. They had fished together just about from when Bevan could walk. He was ready to go off to university now, but he still never knocked back a fishing trip with his dad.

Father and son placed the rods in their holders and settled down to tea and roast-beef sandwiches. They were anchored on what passed as Moondilla's bar, which was a minor thing compared with the bars of some rivers, making it a good place to rest. The water was so shallow that in a good light you could see the sandy bottom.

Sam reckoned that Moondilla was a particularly great fishing spot. There seemed no end to the types of fish you could catch around here. If you wanted real variety, you could go out to the Islands, a group of rocky islets a few miles off shore. On the other hand, if you didn't fancy the big swell, you could fish fairly close in to shore, as Bevan and Sam were doing, or in the river itself. You'd always catch something for dinner.

When they'd had their fill and warmed their bellies, Bevan and Sam threw out with renewed expectation of more flathead. The run-in tide was now taking their lines away, so both men added a bit more lead to keep them from moving too far.

The tide brought all manner of sea creatures into the river, and they hadn't been fishing again long when Bevan declared that he'd hooked something big. Sam looked at the bent rod and, with the wisdom of thirty years' fishing experience, shook his head. 'Naw, I think you're hooked on the bottom.'

Bevan, who was using an expensive lure, admitted that his father was right. 'But I'll go down and see if I can rescue it,' he said.

Sam wasn't too happy about this proposal, given that there were sharks in these waters—but his son was a wonderful swimmer. Bevan handed the rod over to his father, took off his T-shirt and slipped into the water. Sam watched his body, still a bit worried, until it grew formless over the sandbank.

He didn't have to wait long for his son to reappear.

'Dad!' Bevan burst out as he pulled himself onto the launch. 'You won't believe what's down there.' He had to catch his breath.

'What is it?'

Bevan looked like he might be sick. 'There's a woman, a naked woman, and the lure's hooked into her hair.'

Now Sam felt queasy. 'I reckon you don't have to say any more,' he said. 'Jesus, this is a nice kettle of fish. I never heard of anyone going missing.'

'Well, there's a woman down there and she's not a mermaid, Dad.'

●

A few hours later, the divers got her up. She'd been secured with blocks of concrete so that she would never leave the bottom.

She appeared to be a young woman, although her face was badly disfigured. There was no jewellery, tattoos or distinguishing scars, which made her very difficult to identify. The other thing that puzzled the police was why she'd been dumped into relatively shallow water, but they reasoned that the river's mouth was a secluded spot.

Moondilla's medical examiner, Julie Rankin, conducted the autopsy. She pointed to thin, very faint marks across the woman's back, buttocks and thighs. 'If I had to make a guess, I'd say that she's been whipped with a fine leather strap. I found a tiny fraction of leather in her hair at the base of her neck.'

'You think she was into kinky sex?' Inspector Daniels asked, his eyebrow raised. He was the top cop in the district.

'Either she was or the fellow who beat her was,' Dr Rankin said, calm and composed. 'But it was heroin that killed her.'

It seemed that no amount of police work could reveal the woman's name.

And it was from around this time that Moondilla changed in character from a place of very little crime to the centre of drug activities on the South Coast. It began with the sea, and it was the sea and the river that made Moondilla.

CHAPTER ONE

The town of Moondilla was tucked neatly between two promontories that reached out into the vast Pacific Ocean like fat fingers. Within this horseshoe-shaped reach of coastal heath and ivory-hued beaches, there was a river that emptied into and was sustained by the ocean. Protected by the harbour, the river's mouth didn't have the usual bar and wasn't as open to the sea as some other coastal rivers.

On the southern side of the delta, and forming part of the southern promontory, was a tiny beach. A bit farther up from the ocean, a bridge spanned the river, connecting Moondilla to the main highway that wound south towards Victoria.

On the northern or town side of the delta was a broad stretch of sand, usually referred to as Main Beach, and skirting this beach was a wide road that swung in a half-circle to join up with the highway north of Moondilla.

The town's boundary was around two kilometres from its centre and, except for a few farmhouses, the countryside was quite scantily populated. Most people in the area, quite naturally, had clustered around the river and the ocean.

Close by the town was a long wharf or jetty that reached out into the harbour, and at which the fishing trawlers moored to unload their catches. A bitumen road led right up to the jetty so that vehicles could load up with seafood for various markets. There were a couple of smaller jetties southwards of this main one, and here many private launches and yachts were moored.

The road to Sydney provided the greatest number of visitors to Moondilla, but tourists came from everywhere, even from overseas, almost exclusively for the fishing. Even the famous western writer and big-game fisherman Zane Grey had fished this area of the coast, helping to give it an enduring popularity.

Moondilla was also widely regarded as a nice little town for a holiday, being relatively unspoiled by the kind of developments that had changed the character of other coastal towns. For most of its existence, it had had a very low crime rate—but startling new happenings were, to use a marine expression, rocking the boat, and giving the police, both state and federal, cause to put the town under closer scrutiny.

•

It was the most startling of these happenings that occupied Greg Baxter's attention as he drove in to Moondilla. The body of a young woman had been found weighted with concrete blocks not far off the mouth of the river. This horrific discovery had been a boon for the South Coast media, but especially for the Moondilla *Champion*, which ran front-page feature stories for several days. Nothing like this had ever happened in the town and it was, needless to say, the main topic of conversation wherever people met.

It was clearly a case of murder, although the police hadn't revealed any details of the post-mortem. This suggested to Baxter that there were sinister findings which they were reluctant to release to the public, even though they were being pressed to do so.

Baxter's usual sharpness might have been slightly dulled by his preoccupation with the murdered woman, but his reflexes—finely honed by decades of gymnastics and martial arts training—took over when he saw the overturned four-wheel drive. He braked, pulled his car to the side of the road, jumped out and rushed over.

This was well known to be a bad section of road—although the surface was up to standard, the combination of its camber and curve were car killers. The four-wheel drive had hit a tree and flipped onto its side. Baxter peered in the driver's window. Its passengers, a man and a woman, were both alive and semiconscious. Neither was capable of getting out, and both were covered in blood.

Baxter had to lean through the window to turn the ignition off—strong as he was, he couldn't budge the door, which had been partly crushed. By now, a couple of other cars had pulled up, and a driver poked his head out, shouting, 'Need any help?'

'Ambulance,' Baxter called back, 'and have you got any tools on you?'

But none of them had—they were city people out for a jaunt, and they all looked frightened. Heart thumping, Baxter hurried back to his car and riffled through his toolbox for a 'jemmy'. He doubted it was strong enough, but it was the only thing he had that might work.

After a ferocious effort that left his arm strangely numb, he'd just managed to get the driver's door open when the local ambulance arrived with siren blaring, and two paramedics rushed over.

'You've gashed your arm pretty bad there,' said the older ambo. 'Sit down and take it easy, and we'll see about getting this pair out.'

Baxter glanced at his arm, surprised to see the blood dripping down. But, he reasoned, it could wait until they'd rescued the passengers.

CHAPTER TWO

Baxter, his arm wrapped in blood-soaked bandages, was waiting on a chair in the emergency section of Moondilla's medical clinic. The wound didn't trouble him too much—he'd had worse. He was thinking about Moondilla. He'd left the town as a small boy, and one of his strongest memories was of the lovely river that made Moondilla what it was. He'd spent hours watching his father fish off a jetty or from his small runabout.

Baxter hadn't wanted to leave; he'd felt sure there would never be another place as good as Moondilla. But he was only a child and had no say in the matter. Moondilla was the place where his mother, Frances, had begun her culinary career, but she had outgrown it. They'd moved to Sydney, where she'd developed and sold one restaurant after the other, making a heap of money and becoming known to all and sundry as the Great Woman.

Baxter was still thinking about his mother, and how good she'd been to him, when Dr Julie Rankin came through the door.

'My God! Greg Baxter! You're the last man I expected to be treating,' she said when she saw him, and gave him a big smile.

'And it's nice to see you too, Julie,' Baxter said, grinning. She was a sight for sore eyes. They'd parted on very good terms just prior to her going to London for further study. She'd been exceptionally ambitious, with the clear-cut aim of becoming a top surgeon. He had never imagined that she'd come back to Moondilla.

Although they were both from the town, they'd first met in Sydney when Julie had signed up as one of Baxter's martial arts students. She'd set out to reach his level, but he was so far ahead of her that, try as she might, she could never have been in his league. Of course, the fact that he'd been a gymnast of near-Olympic standard gave him an enormous advantage. But he had pushed her quite hard in judo, and she was brown-belt standard when she left him.

'Sorry, Greg,' Julie said, 'I didn't expect to find you here.' She began unfolding his blood-soaked bandages. 'What on earth are you doing in Moondilla?'

'I live here, Julie,' Baxter replied with a half-smile.

'You live here? Where? And for how long?'

'I bought the Carpenter place out on the river. You probably know it.'

Julie nodded, her brow furrowed. She was preoccupied with his bandages, but still seemed to be taking in his words, so Baxter kept talking.

'How long have I been there? A few weeks. I've been pretty busy getting settled in. My mother insisted on me making a few changes to the house. To the kitchen, mainly. That and some glamming up of the main bedroom.'

'Good heavens,' Julie exclaimed.

Baxter couldn't tell whether this remark was made in response to the mention of his bedroom, or because she'd laid bare the wound on his arm.

'This is going to require quite a few stitches,' she said, her eyes wide. 'How on earth did it happen?'

'Well, I reckon I couldn't have anyone better to sew me up, could I?' Baxter said and laughed. 'The last time I saw you was just before you left for Pommyland to specialise in surgery, and knowing you I'd put my money on you doing just that.'

'Greg, how did you come by this?' she asked again, more urgently this time. 'The message just said that there was a man who'd cut his arm rather badly in some sort of accident.'

Baxter shrugged and told her the story.

'I suppose the car could've blown up?' she asked, a stern note in her voice.

'I turned the ignition off first thing, and I was just going to try and get them out when the ambos arrived—I reckon they took the passengers to Bega Hospital—and then the cops showed up. One of them gave me a lift here in my car.' He sighed, thinking of the injured couple and their ruined vehicle, which he'd noticed was filled with holiday gear. 'That's a very bad curve and it needs straightening out. Beats me why it wasn't done years ago.'

Then Baxter realised that Julie had gone very still. 'My brother Andrew was killed on that curve,' she said, her voice trembling slightly although her eyes were dry. 'Andrew and a mate. They'd been to a birthday party. Andrew wasn't driving, and his mate was high as a kite on drugs and took the curve too fast.' She appeared to steel herself before she kept working on Baxter's wound—but then she added, under her breath, 'Andrew was in second-year medicine.'

Baxter knew her better than to try physical comfort, so he just said, 'I'm so sorry to hear that, Julie.'

'It nearly killed my mother. My brother was the apple of her eye.'

'Not you?' Baxter queried, sensing an opportunity to lighten the mood.

Julie rewarded his effort with a half-hearted smile. 'No, not me. Mum and I didn't get on very well in those days. She was jealous that I was so close to Dad. But it was just that she didn't share any of his likes, whereas I did. I'd fish with him for hours at a time . . . Don't move your arm while I give you some local anaesthetic. It will deaden the pain while I stitch up that cut.'

'And now?' Baxter pressed.

'Dad died. That's why I came back to Moondilla. He always wanted either Andrew or me to take over his practice. There was no Andrew, so it had to be me. And I'm getting on quite well now with Mum—she really needed me. Plus there's Jane, my sister, whose kids were in need of an aunt. Two great kids. Sherrie's supposed to be a lot like me at her age—in looks, I mean—and then there's Jason, who's got some problems because he isn't much good at sport.'

Watching Julie's calm face as she told him about her life while concentrating on his wound, Baxter recalled very clearly the first day she'd joined his martial arts class. There were four female students, and Julie was the one who stood out to him. She had a casual beauty that she took for granted and didn't flaunt, as if she was indifferent to it.

She approached him before they started warming up. 'I don't want you to go easy on me because I'm a woman,' she said.

'In my classes everyone gets treated equally,' he told her. 'The fact that you're a woman doesn't concern me one iota. Martial arts is martial arts, though I'll start you on judo at the outset. There's the technique of it and then there's your level of fitness.'

'Well, you'll soon see that I'm very fit and I'm also very tough.'

And she was. He soon learned that she jogged, skydived, did rock climbing and snorkelled. She'd even climbed Kilimanjaro. If there had been a parachute unit for women in the Australian Army, Julie would have had no trouble being accepted for it.

She was also extremely bright, having graduated from medicine with first-class honours.

Julie didn't belong to any feminist organisation, but she was a superlative example of equality between the sexes.

'Why martial arts?' Baxter asked her after a few classes, when they'd gotten to know each other better.

'I hate men making passes at me and I hope to be going places where they'll try more than that. I want to look after myself in tough situations.'

'And why me?' he asked.

'A friend who knew your girlfriend, Elaine, said you were the best in Australia—and that you took small evening classes, which fits in well with my uni hours!'

Baxter also recalled very clearly the day Julie had said goodbye to him.

'This is my final class, Greg,' she said, beaming with gratitude. 'Thank you so much for what you've done for me.'

'No more than for anyone else,' he said, and this was true. He'd made sure not to give her special attention and make her feel uncomfortable.

'Maybe not,' she said, 'but you've helped me build a confidence and a discipline I lacked when I came to you.'

'As I recall it, I doubt you ever displayed a lack of confidence,' he said with a chuckle. 'But that's part of what martial arts is all about.'

'So I'd heard, but I didn't believe it. I was more interested in giving myself an edge if I needed to defend myself.'

'And now?'

'I'm off to the UK to specialise in surgery. National Health has created plenty of opportunities for surgical work,' she explained. 'You know, most top surgeons—most surgeons for that matter—are men. I've got a yen to succeed in that field.'

'Will you keep up your martial arts?' Baxter asked.

'I'll try to, but honestly I don't know. I'm going to be furiously busy.'

So Julie had departed, and he had missed her. She was the only woman, apart from his mother, for whom he felt real affection. She was also the first woman who'd stirred him since he lost Elaine.

'So how did your stint as a surgeon turn out?' Baxter asked while he watched the neat line of stitches flowering on his arm. 'I had visions of you becoming a national figure and ending up in Macquarie Street.'

'Well, I had a good bash at it. And it comes in handy here. I operate at Bega and other places when I have the time.'

'Sounds to me as if you've mellowed quite a lot. You don't appear to be the fire-eater you were when you came to me. You had a lot of aggro in those days.'

'Ha.' She grinned. 'I haven't changed that much, Greg. I'm still regarded as a tough cookie by most people in this district. I disarmed a fellow with a knife and put a hammer lock on him. Those belts I won are in a glass case in my surgery, so everyone's aware that I'm not a pussycat!'

Laughing, Baxter shook his head. 'I'm impressed.' He allowed himself a peek at her body, making sure not to let his eyes linger. She was wearing loose jeans and a comfortable shirt, but he could tell she was still in shape. 'How do you keep fit now?'

She shrugged. 'I jog religiously and I swim when I can.' In the next moment, her professional mask slid back into place. 'You'll probably have a faint scar down your arm, but it will diminish in time. You're lucky we got on to it so early, because these jagged tears become harder to work on the longer they're left.'

She gave Baxter a tetanus shot and some penicillin tablets.

'Take the box,' she said. 'If you have any problems before I remove the stitches, be sure to contact me. And watch out for any red streaks up your arm. Stitches out in, say, twelve days.' She was writing it all down for him. 'It's a long nasty wound and it will be sore when that local wears off. You should get some aspirin so you can sleep tonight. Do you have any questions?'

'Just one. I'll grab the aspirin now, and when your shift is over, meet me for a chat at the coffee place across the street? I'd love to catch up properly.'

Julie's mask slipped and she smiled. 'See you in an hour and a half.'

CHAPTER THREE

After buying aspirin at the chemist next to the clinic, Baxter took a walk up and down the town's main street. Many of the shops and buildings from his childhood were still there, and brought up all kinds of fond memories.

But he also recalled, with painful clarity, the day his mother told him with a smile that they'd soon be leaving Moondilla to live in Sydney.

'But why?' he asked, shocked.

Frances sighed and tried to explain. 'We were offered a very good price for our business, and we took it. Sydney's a bigger market, with so many more people who want to dine out. We've already been offered a place to begin.' She looked thrilled to be leaving their home, and Greg felt even worse.

His face fell. 'But I love it here, Mummy. The beach and the river are my favourite places.'

'Sydney has one of the best harbours in the world, and there's lots of beaches.'

'They'll all be crowded and ugly. It won't be like here.' Greg's throat felt tight and tears stung his eyes. 'The schools will be different too.'

'Greg, you must allow your father and I to be the judges of what's best for our family.' She put her hands on his shoulders and gave them a comforting squeeze, gazing into his eyes. 'I know it's hard for you to understand, but I hope you can trust me. We've gone as far as we can go in Moondilla, and now it's time to move on.'

Greg went away dragging his feet. His mother's announcement was the biggest item of news he'd ever had to digest, and there was only one person he felt disposed to talk to about it. This was the elderly World War One soldier who fished at the southern end of Main Beach, Albert Garland.

Although the young Greg Baxter wasn't then aware of it, Mr Garland had been decorated for gallantry in France. He'd also been gassed and hit by two bullets from a German machine gun. After surviving all of that, he'd lost his son in the Second World War, and then his wife had died when Greg was a baby.

What moved young Greg was that Mr Garland didn't treat him like a little boy, but spoke to him as he did to older people.

Greg had first come across the old man on one of his many tramps around Moondilla. He knew every street of the town, and every nook and cranny, but he was always drawn most to the beaches and the river.

He would sit on the rim of the beach and watch the old man fish, sometimes with a rod and at others a handline. Being a naturally curious little boy, Greg was always interested in the kinds of fish the old man caught. Soon the boy was sitting and watching every day he could, but he kept quiet, afraid that if he caused a disturbance he'd be told to go away.

Finally, after several days of this, the old man spoke to him. 'What's your name, young man?'

'It's Greg. Greg Baxter. We own the restaurant in Moondilla.'

'I'm Albert Garland. You can call me Mr Garland. Like fishing, do you?'

'I like to see the different kinds of fish there are.'

'I suppose you know them all, do you?'

'No, but I know the ones my mum uses in the restaurant. Snapper and flathead mostly.'

'Your mother can't go wrong with them,' Mr Garland said and nodded wisely. 'Very good eating fish. I like them best myself.'

The old man would make lunch of a sandwich and small thermos of tea. He carried them and his fishing gear in an ex-army haversack that had attracted Greg's attention from the outset. Aside from the haversack, Mr Garland carried his rod and a sugar bag with a rope noose. He'd put his catch in the sugar bag and drop it into the water until it was time to leave, when he'd kill and clean the fish.

'That's a strong-looking bag,' Greg said once, after a thorough inspection of the haversack. It was made of a kind of canvas and fastened with brass-edged straps. The boy had never seen a bag like it.

'It will never wear out,' the old man said proudly. 'That haversack was in North Africa. They made them tough for the army.'

•

So it was to Mr Garland that Greg made his way after his mother had told him the awful news. He hoped the old man would appreciate how badly he felt.

'What've you lost, young Greg?' Mr Garland asked. 'You look very down in the mouth.'

'We're leaving Moondilla,' Greg said tremulously. He was on the verge of tears but trying desperately not to appear a sook.

'Ah, so it's true.'

'What do you mean?' Greg asked.

'I heard your people's business had been sold. Surprised me, 'cause it seemed to be going so well.'

'That's the problem.' Greg explained his mum's plans.

Mr Garland listened thoughtfully. 'And you're very unhappy about leaving?'

Greg sniffed. 'Yes, I love this place. I love the beach and the river and watching you fish. I don't want to go to Sydney where there's millions of people.'

'Well, if you're a good boy—and I reckon you are—you'll

fall in with what your people want. They must reckon they're doing the right thing, and it's them that has to find the money for everything. One day it will be your turn to make the decisions about what you're going to do.'

'I suppose so,' Greg said glumly.

The old man set his rod aside and stooped down a bit closer to the boy's level. 'I'll tell you something I've never told anyone—not even my late wife.'

Greg nodded eagerly.

'I was in the first AIF, in France. It was a dreadful business, young Greg. Freezing cold, snow at times, the shelling was awful and the German machine guns were terrible. Then there was their stinking gas. Thousands of Australians killed. I finished up in hospital in England. And do you know what helped to get me through?'

The boy shook his head.

'It was the thought of being able to come back here where there were no guns and no stinking gas, just the sea and the river and the fishing. So I'll give you two pieces of advice. Fall in with a good heart with what your parents want to do, but keep the picture of Moondilla in your mind. And when you're your own boss, you can come back here.'

'What's your second piece of advice, Mr Garland?'

'Be the best it's possible to be at whatever you do. If you're successful, that will help you to come back here.' The old man's face softened in a way the boy had never seen before. 'I'm going to miss you, young Greg. Although I won't be here to see it, I reckon that one day you'll return to Moondilla. That's the kind of young man I think you are. You'll come back here and do things that people remember.'

'But you won't be here,' Greg said, again feeling like he might cry.

Mr Garland shrugged. 'Nobody lives forever. I could have, and probably should have, died in France along with my best mates, so I've had a fortunate reprieve. And I've caught a lot of good fish.'

•

Some three years later, a parcel arrived at the Baxters' home in Sydney, addressed to Greg. It wasn't Christmas or his birthday. 'Who could be sending me a present?'

'If you open it, you'll find out,' Frances said, handing him a pair of scissors.

Once he'd cut the packing tape, Greg tore the cardboard box open and let out a whoop of excitement. 'It's Mr Garland's haversack! It was in North Africa. There's an NX number on it.'

'And there's a note inside,' Frances pointed out.

Greg withdrew the single piece of creamy notepaper.

Dear Greg,
Keep the dream alive.
Your old fishing mate,
Albert Garland.

'He didn't forget,' Greg whispered. 'He knew I liked his haversack.'

'The really worthwhile people never forget, Greg,' his mum told him.

Greg looked at his mother and nodded. Her eyes were damp. That was when he realised that the arrival of the haversack meant Mr Garland had died.

This didn't lessen Greg's desire to go back to Moondilla, though he knew the town would never be quite the same without his friend. An old and very decorated ex-soldier had treated him not as a small boy, but as a mate.

Years later, when he finally returned to live in Moondilla, Baxter brought the haversack with him. In fact, it was where he stowed the aspirin he'd just bought.

CHAPTER FOUR

'So what are *you* doing in Moondilla?' Julie asked, when they were sitting in a corner of the cosy little coffee shop.

He looked down at the long, neat line of stitches in his arm before answering. 'I'm trying to write a book. Although I won't be much good at typing for a while.'

'The great Australian novel?'

'I'll be happy just to get it published,' he said, grinning.

'What's the theme of it?'

'Well, do you remember that journalism was my day job back in Sydney? When I wasn't helping out with one of Mum's cooking ventures.'

Julie nodded.

'I did a couple of big stories about the increase in heroin usage, and the fact that a lot of prostitutes are hooked on it or something equally obnoxious. Mum's publisher was impressed with my work. He said if I ever felt like writing something more substantial, even a novel based on the articles I'd written, he'd be more than happy to have a look. So I've sort of got a foot in the door. Mind you, I've got to produce the book.'

'Hmm. Well, don't tear those stitches.' Julie paused, stirring some sugar into her coffee. 'And is there a Mrs Baxter?'

Baxter caught a glimpse of hope in her eyes—she was probably just hoping that he'd settled down with a nice woman. He wished he could say that he had.

Instead he said, 'I haven't met anyone I wanted to live with. Not after I lost Elaine. And to be honest, not after you left for the UK.' He took a breath and plunged on. 'I have to admit, you were the only woman who appealed to me. But you had other plans. I understood that, and I just hope you never felt I was coming on too strong.'

He thought she might be offended or even angry, but she smiled gently and said, 'There must have been others, Greg. There must have been. Men in your mould don't grow on trees.'

Baxter shook his head. 'Nothing serious. Nothing beyond dinner dates.'

There was a pause as they sipped their coffees.

'So,' she said, just as the silence grew uncomfortable, 'you're out at the Carpenter place on your own and you're writing a book.'

'I'm not entirely on my own.'

'Ah,' she said, her cup clattering as she set it down.

'I have a big dog, Chief. An amazing animal. He's a German Shepherd, bred from imported stock.'

'A dog! You're living on your own with a dog?'

'Yep, is that so hard to believe?'

She gave him a look that told him it was.

'Honestly,' he said and laughed, 'I'm living on a strict budget, keeping up my martial arts routine and working long-ish hours at the computer.'

Julie nodded thoughtfully. 'So you've got a German Shepherd. Things are beginning to click in my head. My sister Jane is dog mad—she has two boxers—and she mentioned that a fellow who came to the garage had a very clever shepherd. You might have met her husband, Steve Lewis. He owns Moondilla Motors.'

'I didn't meet him, just an assistant, but I know him by reputation. He's supposed to be the best mechanic in the district.'

'That's right. He's a decent enough fellow, as men go. Jane could have done a lot worse. His only vice is that he's fishing mad. Mind you, he's not alone around here.'

'It's hardly a vice, Julie,' Baxter protested.

'No, hardly a vice,' she said and smiled. 'Maybe more of an obsession in Steve's case. And to be honest, it's an obsession I understand. Not Jane, though.'

'Steve sounds a nice bloke. And is there anyone I should watch out for?'

She hesitated, then said, her voice low, 'There's one bully boy here: Jack Drew. An ex-pug who slaps his wife around from time to time. It's usually when he's on the booze. I doubt that you'd get on very well with Jack. I've patched up a few fellows he's tangled with, not to mention his gorgeous wife, Liz. You might keep your eyes open for him.'

'You're concerned about my welfare?'

'No, you ninny. I'm concerned about what *you* might do to Jack.'

He tried to look humble, but knew he'd failed when she grinned.

'Anyone else?' he asked.

'There's a Senior Sergeant Cross. Did you meet him at the accident today?'

Baxter shook his head.

'Well, Cross has been here a fair while, and the rumour is that he's bent.'

Baxter cocked an eyebrow. 'Bent in what way?'

Julie's voice lowered even more, and Baxter leaned forward to listen. 'It's said that he's hand in glove with some of the big drug suppliers.'

'Drug suppliers in Moondilla?' he asked harshly.

The discovery of the woman's body had worried Baxter, but he hadn't really believed that the town had fallen so low. Albert Garland would have been horrified.

Baxter's face hardened and his eyes bored into Julie, who looked a little scared. She gestured for him to calm down, and he glanced around, realising that the couple at the table next to them were staring. He made an effort to relax, and Julie kept talking in her soft voice.

'You know we've always had drugs here—'

'But only in a low-key kind of way.'

'Yes, that's true.' Her mouth was drawn tight, and he realised she might be thinking of her brother. 'Now there seems little doubt that drugs are being landed here from the sea and then sent on to Sydney and Melbourne. The locals are reluctant to talk about it—they remember what happened to Donald Mackay in Griffith.'

Baxter shook his head. 'I hate the whole drug scene, Julie,' he said bleakly. 'I knew people who got hooked on drugs. Someone who died. It's what I'm writing about. I hate drugs and I hate the people pushing them.' It was a huge effort to keep his voice down. 'As far as I'm concerned, anyone who pushes drugs is a complete mongrel, the lowest kind of person on this earth. It's a rotten business.'

'I agree. Drugs and alcohol have a lot to answer for. My brother's death, for one.'

Baxter nodded, wishing there was something he could do or say to comfort her.

'And now,' she added, a quaver in her voice, 'it's my job to deal with the consequences of those things every week of my life.'

They'd finished their coffee and Baxter wasn't sure what else to say—just that he wanted to see her again. But now, after everything she'd told him, and with the new weight on his mind, it was difficult to ask.

He was relieved when she beat him to the pleasantries. 'It's really good seeing you again, Greg,' she said, making an effort to smile. 'It gave me a shock seeing you sitting there. I hope you have a very pleasant sojourn in Moondilla, despite its problems.'

'Thanks, I plan on being here quite a while.' This was his chance. 'I hope you'll come out and see me—I'll cook you a decent fish meal.'

He'd hoped he sounded casual enough, but Julie raised her eyebrows and said sharply, 'You should know that I'm not looking for a relationship.'

'Who said anything about a relationship? I didn't have that in mind.'

But the barriers were up. 'Men always have that in mind.'

'Look, it's a very agreeable spot, and you can fish off my jetty if you'd like. Or we can go out on the small runabout I bought with the place. She's named the *Flora Jane* after old Harry's grandma.'

It was the right thing to say. Julie's face softened, and she looked a little embarrassed, colour rising in her cheeks. 'Sorry, Greg. That does sound lovely. My dad had a fishing boat too—an area of dispute between him and Mum.' She swallowed. 'When he died, she sold the boat.'

Baxter felt a surge of sympathy—Julie had certainly been through the ringer. 'That's a shame,' he said. 'Well, there you are, you can come and fish with me. I'll bet you could teach me a lot.'

'We'll see.' She got to her feet, a grin back on her face. 'You get on home now, have a cup of tea and something to eat, and take a couple of those aspirin. And don't be a bad patient. Take the antibiotics!'

'Yes, Dr Rankin, whatever you say.' He chuckled and glanced at his arm as he stood up. 'And thanks for the embroidery. When I left for Moondilla, I didn't imagine I'd be returning with a sample of your handiwork.'

CHAPTER FIVE

Baxter smiled to himself as he pulled up the driveway to his riverside home. He hadn't been there long, but already he had a great fondness for the place. He'd never experienced any warm feelings towards the apartments he'd rented in Sydney. Riverview was different—it was beautiful, and it was his own.

He also had a great warmth for his mother, who'd helped him buy the property. Frances wouldn't have done it if she'd disapproved—she was a shrewd businesswoman as well as a renowned chef—but the fact was that she liked Riverview and believed it was a good buy. Her trusted real estate valuer had assured her that the property was likely to appreciate greatly in the very near future. Sydney businesspeople were buying up South Coast land and either renovating farmhouses or building flash new homes, and some were commuting to and from the city by helicopter.

The Riverview house was getting long in the tooth, Frances had said, and might be best knocked down and replaced. But Baxter didn't mind it. The lovely old building was on a slight rise, and its park-like surrounds were dotted with many varieties of shrubs and trees. There were bougainvillea vines and jacarandas, and two pergolas draped with mauve and white wisteria. The empty poultry yards and a large garage and storage shed were almost smothered by passion fruit and honeysuckle.

At the back of the house was a netted vegetable garden that still contained some of the many vegetables the last owner, Harry Carpenter, had lovingly tended into his old age. Silver-beet and rhubarb were still thriving, and there were drums holding parsley, mint and other herbs. How the Great Woman's eyes had gleamed when she saw all these plants and a great bin of developing compost.

While the house wasn't young, it was made of sturdy timber. Baxter didn't want to do any major external work, at least for the moment, but he'd agreed with his mother that it would look better for a coat of paint and a few minor repairs.

As he'd said to Julie, there'd been a lot of internal work done, and the kitchen had been fully renovated at his mum's insistence. She'd declared the old kitchen a disaster—quite unsuitable for the preparation of high-quality meals. She hadn't yet seen the finished product, but Baxter was certain she wouldn't be disappointed. A large new electric range had replaced the stove, and Baxter had added a gas-fired stove that could be utilised when there were electricity blackouts. These stoves, along with gleaming sinks, preparation tables and cupboards, had transformed the room.

A large verandah wrapped around the whole house. On the side facing the river, Baxter had placed one of the tables he'd brought from Sydney. He liked to sit there as the sun dipped behind the mountains to the west. Birds of many varieties flew up and down the river before roosting in the trees on both banks.

The atmosphere was so intoxicating for someone used to the hustle and bustle of Sydney as to threaten to drown his senses and seriously erode his hours of writing. The earlier mornings were, if anything, even headier, with life returning to the river as the sun came up over the great ocean to the east.

As Riverview's name implied, it was the river that contributed the most to the property's appeal. High grassy banks overlooked the tranquil water. Though smaller than some rivers along the NSW North Coast, it was still a considerable body of water and as changeable as life itself. Something was always happening on the river, even if it was only a fish jumping in an arc of flashing silver.

The river was tidal, of course, and still full of salt at Riverview, but it became brackish as it approached the mountains. Even so, old hands swore that they'd seen bull sharks some miles up from Baxter's jetty, which seemed to dispose of the theory that the predators couldn't survive in anything but salt water.

These shark stories added some spice, tempered by caution, to Baxter's view of the river. He didn't go swimming from his jetty, and kept Chief out of the water too. The German Shepherd took a dim view about being landlocked; he liked to paddle after ducks, which he felt had no right to be swimming close to *his* jetty. Chastised for going in the river, Chief would lie at the jetty's edge and stare malevolently at the ducks as they floated, indolent, on the gently moving water.

There was a world of difference between how Greg, as a young boy, had viewed the river, and how Baxter saw it now. But the river still answered all his questions and fulfilled the dreams he'd had of it.

•

Next morning Baxter got up at dawn as usual and went jogging with Chief. He talked to the German Shepherd just as if he were human—and Baxter was almost certain that Chief understood everything he said.

Baxter was on a high about Chief. He'd never owned a dog before, though he'd long wanted one. His lifestyle just hadn't been conducive to dog ownership, but making the decision to buy a property with some acres had changed that.

Nearly two years ago, when he hadn't yet found the time to start looking for the right place, one of his mother's wealthy friends happened to import a pair of German Shepherds and breed a litter from the bitch. The dogs were intensively tested for hip dysplasia: a curse of the breed, initiated to some extent by show breeders selecting dogs for greater angulation. Once the pups were in the clear, Baxter had booked one and made his selection when they were about eight weeks old. He'd moved into an apartment with a courtyard where the growing pup had some space to roam.

Baxter's decision to purchase a German Shepherd was no hit-or-miss judgement. He'd looked at all the major dog breeds before narrowing them down to three that stood out for general usefulness: the border collie, kelpie and German Shepherd. The third breed wasn't 'worky' like the other two, but Baxter didn't need a working-type dog. What he wanted was one with high intelligence and the ability to be taught—and one with a certain presence. The Labrador could certainly be taught, but didn't fit his concept of what a dog should be, so it came down to kelpie versus shepherd.

Baxter could never forget the story his father had told him about Zoe the white German Shepherd, handled by the legendary police trainer Sergeant 'Scotty' Denholm. Zoe had been fitted with a special radio transmitter strapped to her back. From high in a stand at the Sydney Showground, Denholm had transmitted instructions to her on the oval below. This was the kind of temperament Baxter was looking for in a dog.

Now, with Chief fully grown and losing his puppyish nature, Baxter was delighted with his choice. The dog was noble in character and a great mate—and he was *super* smart.

Nobody could get near the house without the shepherd letting Baxter know.

Chief was on the lookout for all kinds of intruder. A few days after moving in, Baxter had been sitting at his table on the verandah when he'd heard a low growl. He'd glanced up to see the hairs rise on Chief's withers. The dog's attention was focused on something across the lawn—a black snake, gliding towards the sanctuary of a clump of low shrubs.

Baxter couldn't risk the snake taking up permanent residence and perhaps biting Chief, so he'd killed it with a shovel while the shepherd growled fiercely from behind him. It seemed Chief knew instinctively that snakes were bad medicine.

•

After breakfast, Baxter did a couple of hours' research on drugs for his novel, and then took a cup of tea and a tomato sandwich out to the verandah. Chief, as usual, came and sat beside him. Baxter put down the cup and flexed his arm. It was still aching a little, despite the two aspirin he'd taken, but Julie's stitches remained pristine.

As he sipped his tea, Baxter gazed at the river and thought, for the umpteenth time, how fortunate he'd been to acquire this property. It offered so much more than he could have purchased for the same money in—or anywhere near—Sydney. Sure, he didn't have an ocean or harbour view, but to him the river was even better.

The river crept quite high at times, but the Carpenters had lived on the property for most of their long lives and the water had never even reached the verandah. That's what old Harry had told the Baxters, and it was backed up by their solicitor. However, for some reason the old chap had wanted a quick sale and accepted less than the property's market value. Frances had joked that the place must be haunted.

His belly full, Baxter decided to give the indoor work away for an hour or so. After what Julie had told him, reading about drugs was making him feel even worse than it usually did. He needed to take his mind off things, so he walked down to the jetty and baited two lines—one with dough and cotton wool, the other with a piece of mullet. Today he was after a flathead, the tastiest of the fish he'd caught so far; but he'd found he could make a first-class meal of almost any kind of fish, even yellow-eye mullet.

Baxter was still coming to grips with fishing. Until he'd moved back here, his only experiences with it had been watching his dad and Mr Garland. Now a whole new world was opening up for him. To identify his catches, he'd purchased a second-hand copy of Jack Pollard's 950-page *Complete Guide to Australian Fishing*.

He'd caught a variety of fish close to the river's mouth, but so far he hadn't ventured out farther. He recognised that he didn't have the expertise to handle a boat on the ocean, especially around the Islands. Not on his own, anyway.

Inside an hour he'd hooked a good-sized flathead and then a fish he hadn't caught before. A perusal of Pollard's book identified it as a King George whiting, arguably the most highly prized fish of southern Australian waters, and a variety that rarely travelled this far north. Baxter was chuffed about that—as a chef, the prospect of trying something new stirred his senses. He cleaned both fish and put them in his Esky.

He reckoned he'd have an hour at his desk before lunch, and had put in perhaps half an hour when Chief looked up at him and barked. He knew that bark. It was to warn him that a vehicle was coming up the track from the road.

CHAPTER SIX

Baxter got up and went out on the verandah, shielding his eyes against the sun to take a look at the vehicle. He didn't get many callers and wasn't expecting anyone today, but that didn't mean anything in the country. You could get a Rawleigh's rep any old time. People simply took it for granted that they'd be welcome. And they mostly were.

But because of what Julie had told him, Baxter was wary. This wasn't a Rawleigh's or any other kind of rep. The vehicle was a rather shabby, putty-coloured panel van. He'd noticed it—and its similarly shabby-looking male driver—at various places in the district since his arrival in Moondilla. The driver was a self-proclaimed artist, often to be observed painting at Main Beach.

When the van pulled up, the driver climbed out with a wave. He wasn't a badly built bloke, but his appearance didn't flatter him. His long fair hair was tied in a ponytail and his clothes had clearly never come in contact with an iron. Not only that, but the jeans were holey in places, and the shirt was mottled with splotches of different-coloured paint. There was a generous streak of blue down his left forearm.

'G'day,' he called with a wide smile, sounding a bit too familiar, as he walked up to the verandah. 'Great afternoon, isn't it?'

Baxter was cautiously polite. 'It certainly is. How can I help you?'

'I've been talking to Dr Rankin. She told me you were here. How's the arm?'

Why had a bloke like this been talking to Julie? And it seemed she'd broken doctor–patient confidentiality: that didn't sound like her. Baxter tensed. 'It's still a bit sore, but not too bad. So you know Dr Rankin?'

'Only professionally, champ. I'm Ian Latham.' He held out a paint-stained hand, but Baxter didn't shake it, so he shrugged and gestured to Chief, whose hackles were raised. 'That's a great-looking shepherd.' And in the next breath. 'Could we have a yarn?'

'Sorry, I'm writing right now. Or trying to. Is it important?'

'Dr Rankin suggested I should meet with you. She considered it important. You'd trust her judgement, wouldn't you?'

Baxter had to agree that he would, although he was still worried she'd been coerced somehow. 'Did she? You'd better come in. Fancy a drink of something . . . tea or coffee?'

'Coffee, if it's not too much trouble. Tea, if it is.'

Baxter sat his visitor down in the lounge room, handed him a fishing journal and went to make coffee. Chief lay in the doorway and watched Latham with unblinking interest: the paint smells on this new human's clothes were an interesting development.

When Baxter came back with two steaming mugs, he took a seat opposite Latham, and Chief came to lie at his feet.

'The thing is,' Latham began, 'I'm not really an artist.'

Alarmed, Baxter tensed again, and Latham hurried to reassure him.

'Well, I am, but it's not my occupation, just a hobby.' He smiled disarmingly. 'I'm a detective sergeant with the drug squad, and right now I'm working undercover. I don't carry identification for obvious reasons.'

Allowing himself to relax a little, Baxter said, 'I see. And what are you doing in this area?' He'd keep what Julie had told him up his sleeve until he learned what it was that Latham wanted. Play a bit dumb. Plus, given what she'd said about Senior Sergeant Cross, Baxter needed to be as sure as possible that the man could be trusted.

'As you're probably aware, drugs are coming into Australia in many different ways and at many different places. We reckon that some have come in through Moondilla, and we're fairly certain more will be landed here very soon.'

'You know that for a fact?' Baxter asked, a chill in his voice. Chief lifted his head.

'We're as sure as we can be. Most of the attention has been on the North Coast and Queensland, but some of the rotten stuff has come in down here.'

This was exactly what Baxter didn't want to hear: Moondilla still looked idyllic, but it was tainted. And this was the place that Mr Garland had been proud to call home.

Baxter steeled himself. 'Where do I come into the picture?'

'There's things you don't know but should,' Latham said. 'Harry Carpenter was contacted by certain persons because of his good jetty and those sheds behind your house. Harry, as you may have judged, is a man of the old school, very honest and upright, and he wouldn't have a bar of their proposition. He confided in the only person he reckoned he could trust—'

'Jul—Dr Rankin.'

'Yes. Harry had known her dad, been treated by him for years. A true blue bloke.'

'Why didn't Harry trust the police?'

'There's a sergeant here he couldn't stomach—Cross, Ron Cross. He booked Harry for some minor problem when he could have given him a caution. After that, the old bloke wouldn't go near the police.' Latham leaned closer and his voice lowered. 'Between you and me, and as much as it pains me to tell you, we have a strong suspicion that Cross is on the take.'

This tallied with what Julie had said. Baxter reckoned he'd continue to play dumb and extract the maximum amount of information. 'You mean he's bent?'

'Yes, exactly. We think he's passing information about our movements to the drug distributors. He thinks he's pretty clever, but—' Latham smiled wryly '—he doesn't know that I'm an undercover cop. He also doesn't know we're on to him.'

'So why did you tell me? I could spill the beans.'

'Dr Rankin said I could trust you.'

'How come you're so close to her?' Baxter asked, not quite managing to keep the proprietary note out of his voice.

Latham grinned. 'In the first place, Dr Rankin is the medical examiner and does most of the autopsies in this area. She's a very smart cookie, is our Doc.'

Baxter wondered what Julie would have made of that description.

'Secondly,' Latham continued, 'I had a bad bout of diarrhoea from eating rough food while I was on a surveillance job, and I had to go to her. I asked if any of her patients were addicts, and she said yes, but of course she wouldn't breach their confidentiality. But now she's breached it for you—she's concerned about you being out here. She asked me to warn you that you might receive some unwelcome visitors.'

'So you reckon those same fellows will contact me.'

Latham nodded. 'You've got the best jetty—best all-weather jetty—from here to the mouth of the river. They could unload the rotten stuff here, store it in your sheds, then pick it up and drive to the big smoke—and there's no close neighbours to watch them. No matter what, they need somewhere to land that's not in the public eye.'

It sounded straightforward enough, but something still didn't make sense. Baxter frowned. 'Wouldn't a yacht appear a bit conspicuous if it came chugging to my jetty?'

'They'd trans-ship at sea, maybe to a fishing trawler, or a smaller yacht or launch. You've probably seen quite a few launches go past your jetty. Any one of those could belong to the drug mob. They aren't short of a quid.'

Baxter had certainly noticed launches on the river. He was gradually identifying the locals, but there'd been many strangers too. Some headed for the river's upper-reaches to fish for bass. He hadn't thought anything of it; now it turned his stomach.

There was another thing he needed to confirm. 'This young woman that's just been fished out of the water. I read about her in the local paper. How did she die?'

'Dr Rankin did the autopsy: a massive heroin overdose. But I didn't tell you that, so keep it to yourself.'

'The paper said her identity was unknown.'

Latham looked away and sipped his coffee, appearing to consider what to reveal—then he shrugged. 'I've told you about Cross, so I may as well let you in on the truth about this too. That's not the way it is. The murdered woman was an extremely courageous member of the drug squad. She volunteered to go all the way as a prostitute in order to give us a closer handle on the drug business.'

It took a few seconds for Baxter to take that in. And he'd thought he was sickened before. 'How on earth did she manage it?'

'She'd lost her sister to drugs a few months before, so she was prepared to risk her own life to get the info we needed.' Latham's voice had roughened. 'They must have tumbled to her. She wouldn't have had a good end. She'd had a beating, and the big boss of this operation is into kinky sex. Nice fellow.' Latham cleared his throat. 'One day, when we've locked up all the scum, she'll receive a posthumous decoration.'

They were silent for a moment. Baxter realised his coffee had gone cold.

'This sounds like a fair-sized operation,' he said.

'It is. Apart from our state drug squad, there's the federal police and customs. Certain people are within close call. Don't let the appearance of my van deceive you.'

'So what have you got in mind for me?' Baxter asked. He wanted to help however he could, but he hated the thought of going anywhere near the drug scene.

'You've got two choices if they approach you,' Latham said, with a rather grim sort of smile. 'You could tell them to get stuffed—or you could go along with them and then report to me.'

'Nix to the latter,' Baxter said vehemently, and Chief gave a low growl. 'I could be accused of being part of their chain. They could even blackmail me later on. No thanks. I'd tell them to piss off and leave me alone.'

'That's what I thought you'd say. I wouldn't think that a fellow in your mould would agree to drugs being landed here, and I can't make you co-operate.'

Baxter held up a hand. 'Whoa, hang fire, Geronimo. I didn't say I wouldn't co-operate. I'll let you know if those creeps contact me.'

'That would be a help,' Latham said, sounding relieved, 'and if they do contact, it might suggest that the next cargo isn't far away, which is in line with our thinking.'

Hell's bells, Baxter thought. He'd wanted to write about Sydney's drug-related hijinks in peace, and now he found himself in a danger zone. With a wry grin, he said, 'I couldn't understand why this property was such a bargain. It seemed too good to be true—and when that happens, there's usually a fly in the ointment.'

Latham chuckled. 'Too right.'

'So how do I get in touch with you?'

He took out a notepad and pen, and wrote down a phone number. 'This is a special number for re-routing calls. You needn't give your name. Simply tell them: "Southern delivery for L".'

'Southern delivery for L,' Baxter repeated.

'Either me or someone else from the team will call you back, or be here to see you not long after you make that call. And if they come calling, you won't touch them, will you?'

'What makes you think I'd do that?'

Latham smiled thinly. 'I understand from Dr Rankin that you're one of the best exponents of martial arts in Australia— maybe even the world. Black belts galore. I don't doubt that you could handle a couple of crims.'

'Well now, Detective Sergeant, I won't make any promises. If they don't touch me, I won't touch them.'

'That's what I thought. I wouldn't blame you for defending yourself.' Latham paused. 'There's something else I should tell you.'

'I knew I hadn't heard it all.'

'There's a fellow living in these parts who we think might be Mr Big. His name's Franco Campanelli. He's got a finger in a lot of pies, and he owns two fishing trawlers and a very swish yacht. You might have noticed him around town. He drives a blue Mercedes and is seldom seen without the company of his two goons.'

'I see. I don't know him, but I don't know many of the locals. I only go to town for my tucker and Chief's meat.' Baxter realised he had another question. 'I was warned about someone, though. Do you know anything about Jack Drew?'

'Yeah.' Latham's expression turned contemptuous. 'Drew is of no account. He knocks his wife about when he gets on the piss, but she won't dob him in. No, the drug boys wouldn't involve a yobbo like Drew. He'd be too unreliable.'

Baxter nodded. 'Figures. I just wondered if there was more to him than that.'

'Not unless he's a bloody marvellous actor.' Setting his empty mug on the coffee table, Latham got to his feet. 'Well, I'd best head off. Urgent beachscapes to paint.'

'No worries.' Baxter stood up too, and they shook hands.

Just as he was going out the door, Latham turned to Baxter and said, 'Off the record, do you own any firearms?'

'Only my father's old shotgun. Why?'

'Hide it, but put it where you can get your hands on it if you need to. Remember that even a martial arts champion can't beat a bullet.'

'I'll remember that,' Baxter said.

Latham nodded. 'Thanks for the great coffee and for lending me some of your time. And good luck with your writing. If you see or hear anything suspicious, get in touch quick and lively.'

Baxter put his hand over his heart and grinned. 'I promise.'

With a heavy heart, he watched Latham's van go down the track. It was obscene that Moondilla's tranquillity was being undermined by a drug ring. He just hoped that Latham and Company would clean them up before long—and he was totally confident that in the meantime he could handle any drug emissary.

CHAPTER SEVEN

Soon after Latham headed off, Baxter changed his clothes. Wearing only a pair of white shorts and his gym shoes, he went out to the biggest of the two sheds behind the house. One corner had been cleared of everything Harry Carpenter had left behind, and the floor laid with a large tarpaulin.

Here, for an hour every day, Baxter went through his martial arts and gymnastic routines. Chief lay against one wall and half-slept, with an eye always on his master.

Today Baxter was only halfway through when the shepherd growled and then gave two warning barks. This usually meant there was a vehicle at the gate. Baxter went to a small crack in the wall of the shed and applied one eye to it.

The car was white, and when its driver got out to close the gate, he was pretty sure it was Julie Rankin.

'Stiffen and starve the beetles, this place is getting like Pitt Street,' Baxter muttered. 'Go and meet her, Chief—she's friendly.'

The dog trotted outside and Baxter went back to his exercises. Presently he saw that Julie, escorted by Chief, had entered the shed. He walked across to her and she gave him a half-smile. 'I didn't expect to see you again so soon, Julie,' he said, smiling.

'Is that the way you rest your arm?' she asked by way of greeting.

He glanced down, realising he'd forgotten all about it. 'I've been careful. I'm not hitting anything.'

'Hmm.' She ran her eyes over him. 'I must say you still look terrific. You haven't put on any weight.'

There was nothing sexual about it, Baxter told himself— she'd always been in awe of his physique and prowess.

'Nor, I observe, have you,' he countered. He thought she looked very trim today in a tan shirt and cream blouse. She was wearing low-heeled shoes that matched her shirt, and from what he could see of her legs they were in good shape.

'Liar,' she said, laughing. 'I *have*, Greg. I don't get the chance to exercise like I should. Being a doctor uses up most of my time.'

Greg towelled himself off and pulled on a loose old T-shirt. 'Not too busy to take me up on my invitation, I see.'

'Well, knowing you, I thought I'd better come out here and look at your arm. And I was right!'

They walked together out of the shed and towards the house, Chief following close at Baxter's heels.

'By the way,' Julie said, much more hesitant than usual, 'I asked a detective by the name of Ian Latham to call on you.'

'He's been. He came this morning.'

'I hope you don't mind me asking him to drop by. Did he explain everything?'

Baxter nodded, and Julie's brow furrowed.

'I had no idea it was you who had bought this place. Harry simply said that he'd sold it to a Sydney fellow.'

'It's okay, Julie. Latham put me in the picture. If those fellows call on me, I'll tell them to get lost and that will be that. I'd have bought the place no matter what. It was too good a buy to ignore.' He gestured to the beautiful old house and its overgrown garden as they reached the verandah. 'Now I know why.'

•

When Baxter had made a pot of tea, they sat down together in the living room. Julie poured the steaming liquid while he struggled to think of what to say.

The words finally came to him. 'You know, if I hadn't been so keen to get started on my book, I would've made some enquiries about your whereabouts. It was in the back of my mind—I've always wondered where you'd end up.'

She half-smiled and looked down at her tea. 'Really?'

'Really,' he said. 'Putting aside my feelings for you at the time, you were my most interesting student. You had a lot of aggro in you, and a lot of ambition too.'

'Well, you did me a lot of good, Greg. Calmed me down. But I thought you were completely devoted to martial arts—I had no idea you wanted to write.'

'You knew I was a journalist.'

'Yes, but I thought it was just a job. Not that we talked a great deal about our aspirations.' She looked around at the comfortably furnished room. 'You never seemed to care very much about making money, and I understand there was a fair bit on this place, even though it was a good deal. It didn't seem the kind of thing you'd do.'

Until now, Baxter hadn't wanted to tell Julie about his mum's help, but now this seemed foolish. Julie wouldn't care—she might even find it reassuring.

'I've been saving for years,' he said, 'but the fact is that Mum gave me a fair lump of what this place cost. She wouldn't entertain the idea of me taking out a mortgage for it. She likes it here, and she said that the quicker I got the writing out of my system, the quicker I might settle down and give her some grandchildren.'

Julie laughed. 'Sounds like my mother.'

'*Every* mother,' he said, with a fond laugh. 'Mum has just about everything but the daughter she always wanted and some grandkids. I'm her only hope, and she won't allow me to forget it.'

'I see,' said Julie, sobering. 'Well, I'm sure that as a drug-pusher magnet, this place isn't exactly what Frances envisioned. But at least you know the score now.'

'I'm not at all concerned.' He didn't want to dwell on it, so he started clearing away the tea things. 'I'm going to take a shower now, and then eat lunch. Stay and have some with me?'

'I wouldn't be intruding?'

'Of course not.' He hoped he didn't sound too eager. 'I can offer you something pretty special. I caught what I think is an errant King George whiting, so you can have a fillet of that—or some flathead, if you'd rather. Or both. I'll throw in a hollandaise sauce and some salad. How does that sound?'

She beamed. 'Much tastier than my usual sandwiches. I just hope I don't get called back in before I'm able to sample your expertise.'

•

Julie looked around the renovated kitchen with its new electric and Aga stoves. 'Old Harry wouldn't recognise it now,' she said, leaning against a polished bench.

'Mum's doing.' Greg started pulling out the ingredients. 'She said I couldn't expect a modern young woman to put up with an old kitchen.'

He met Julie's eyes and they both burst out laughing.

'Mum's always about three moves ahead of everyone else. The fact that I don't have a girlfriend, modern or otherwise, doesn't matter to her. The kitchen is ready for when I do have one.' He put tomatoes and a cucumber on a chopping board and set a knife beside it. 'Slice these up while I look after the fish?'

Julie nodded and picked up the knife. She was a little clumsy with it, as though performing surgery, so he demonstrated his technique before he started on the fish.

'I was feeling a wee bit sorry for you,' she said wryly, 'living out here on your own. Not any longer.'

He tossed the fish in the pan and shot her a grin. 'I'm not on my own. I have Chief —he's almost human. And I ought to be able to cook after serving an apprenticeship with the Great Woman. Anyway, cooking doesn't call for a surgeon's skill. I'd never be able to come at your caper. The thought of cutting into a person makes my blood run cold. Well, you know what I mean.'

'I know what you mean. Each to his or her own, and I've been close to medicine ever since I was a child.'

Julie set the kitchen table while Baxter plated the fish. As they sat down opposite each other, he returned Julie's pleased smile and reflected on how glad he was that Frances had insisted on renovating the kitchen.

With one bite, Julie declared the meal delicious, and she polished off every bit of it. They were drinking orange juice and, after they'd finished eating, Baxter filled up her glass and suggested they adjourn to his favourite spot on the verandah. There, beside a large purple bougainvillea, they sat in cane chairs and looked out across the river.

'I can understand why a writer would like this place,' Julie said. 'Some writers, anyway. I met a few while in the UK—both far out in the country and right in London. I gleaned that some like to live close to the heart of things, while others prefer solitude. But wasn't it Tolstoy who said that a writer needs to be close to the soil?'

'So the story goes,' Baxter said. 'And that's true for me. Not that I can really describe myself as a writer yet. As you pointed out, being a journalist isn't quite the same thing. I've always wanted to write but never had the time or money. Mum helped me, and now I'm here. She thinks it's another phase and that I'll get over it.' He paused and met Julie's gaze. 'I don't want to get over it.'

'My mother's said similar things to me. Many times.'

'Well, mum's always been there for me, and although she hasn't always agreed with what I've done, she's tried to understand why I've done them. She certainly understood why I was so down in the dumps after Elaine died. We were going to get married after we came back from overseas, and that meant Mum would get her grandchildren. So, no daughter-in-law, no grandchildren.'

A sympathetic look came into Julie's eyes. 'You never told me anything about Elaine, other than you lost her. Was it so bad an experience that you don't want to talk about her?'

'It was altogether too bad an experience. The whole thing seemed so unfair. We'd planned on doing so much together—' He broke off.

Julie laid a hand on his arm. 'It's all right, I understand. You don't have to say anything more.'

'No, it's been years. I can talk about her now.' Baxter cleared his throat. 'We met in our last year at high school and hit it off straight away. We were both going to study journalism, and we had great plans to head overseas after graduation. I'd get a chef's position in Paris or London, and we'd explore Europe.'

Julie squeezed his arm and he gave her a grateful half-smile.

'I was into gymnastics and martial arts, and Elaine was very outdoorsy. She used to run with me. But then . . .' He swallowed. 'In our second year at uni, she started having trouble keeping up with me. I told her to get a check-up, but unbeknown to me, she'd already had some tests. She didn't want to tell me what they revealed.'

'Cancer.'

Baxter nodded. 'Leukaemia. It was pretty severe and she went downhill fast. Nothing did any good. When she died, I felt the world had come to an end. All our dreams were gone. I was going to chuck university—but Mum, good old Mum, said that was the last thing Elaine would have wanted me to do.'

Julie gave his arm one last squeeze, then slid her hand away. Its warmth lingered.

For some reason, Baxter wanted to keep talking about Elaine, even though it was painful. 'The thing was, Elaine was a mate. We did almost everything together and had long talks. Of course I found her attractive—she was a beautiful blonde girl with a great smile. But she stood out from all the others. There was nothing small about her.'

Julie was the same, Baxter thought, as he looked at the woman beside him. She wasn't so much like Elaine, but she stood out just as Elaine had.

Then he realised he'd been staring at her without saying anything, maybe for a little too long. He quickly glanced away.

'It sounds like Elaine had a great attitude to life,' Julie said.

'She did. I was lucky to meet her, even though we weren't together very long. She sort of set the standard for a girlfriend. That's about the size of it, Julie.'

'Thank you. I can see you don't like talking about it, even now.'

'I wouldn't talk about it to just anyone.'

They sipped their juice without taking their gaze from the river.

Eventually Julie put her glass down on the little table beside her chair. 'Greg, I want to thank you, belatedly, for what you did for me. No, don't stop me. I was really uptight when I went to you. I was ready to take on every man in sight. You were very kind and never tried anything. Other fellows did try. It's the price a woman pays for having looks and a decent figure, and I thought martial arts was the answer.'

'You certainly seemed very troubled.'

'I was.' Her expression smoothed out, and she had a faraway look in her eyes.

He hoped she'd tell him more, especially after all he'd just said about Elaine.

She focused back on him. 'What really bugs me,' she said, 'is that so many people won't accept that a man and a woman can just be friends. If I keep coming out here, everyone will say we're having an affair. But I'd like to go out fishing with you on a regular basis—just as a friend.'

CHAPTER EIGHT

'Would you?' asked a stunned Baxter. This was the first time Julie had reached out to him in any way. The longer he thought about it, the more stunned he was.

'Yes, I would,' she said. 'When I needed a man I could trust—I mean, apart from my dad—you were there for me, and I don't think you've changed.'

'But look, Julie, as much as I respect you for the dedication you showed as my student, and as much as I admire what you've achieved professionally, the basic fact remains that . . .' He didn't know how to put it delicately.

Her eyebrows lifted. 'You're still attracted to me?'

He laughed in relief. 'Of course I am.'

But Julie wasn't laughing. 'It always gets back to sex.'

'It's not as bad as you think. I can't help how I feel—if men didn't feel that way about women, the world would come to a halt—but you can come fishing with me any time you want. I won't promise not to look, but I'll never lay a finger on you, or say anything to make you uncomfortable.'

She considered this.

'It'll be the same as when you were my student,' Baxter added, 'except this time you're the expert.'

'All right, I see what you mean.'

'You'd have to give me the green light before I'd start anything,' he said with a smile, and finally she smiled back.

Julie was definitely reaching out to him, he reckoned—not for sex, obviously, but for something she hadn't experienced since the death of her father. She wanted a mate.

He saw that her eyes were on him, but she didn't speak.

'I thought about you quite a lot, Julie,' he confessed. 'I reckoned you could do almost anything if you set your mind to it. To be honest, I was shocked to find you back here. Not that Moondilla isn't a lovely place to live, but not for the Julie Rankin I knew.'

'I told you why I came back,' she said quickly.

'Sure you did. Your people needed you and you came.' He leaned a bit closer and spoke more gently. 'And maybe, just maybe, the anger burned out, and being close to your people was more important than your ambition.'

'True enough.' That faraway look was creeping back into her eyes.

'Well,' he said, giving her a reassuring grin, 'I'm very pleased you're here—because I need all the help with fishing I can get.'

The mood lightened. Julie smiled and got to her feet, picking up their glasses. 'I'm not the best, but I do know a fair bit about it.'

'I'm just a rank amateur who could use some expert help. I've gained most of my knowledge from books and magazines.'

'If I can catch 'em, you can certainly cook 'em,' Julie said and laughed. 'I'll have to be going, Greg—I'm due back at the clinic. Thanks for the lovely lunch. And be careful with that arm!'

He put on a mock-solemn expression. 'Yes, Dr Rankin, I'll try to.'

As she was walking to the front door, Julie bent down to give Chief a scratch behind the ears.

'Almost forgot to ask,' Baxter said, 'is there a vet in Moondilla? Chief's due for a parvo and distemper.'

'A vet. Yes, there's a vet. She's young, attractive and . . . well, unmarried.'

Baxter chuckled. 'For goodness sakes, Julie. Don't tell me you're in league with my mother, trying to push me into marriage?'

They both laughed.

'Is she also a good vet?' he asked.

'Yep. Sarah Morrison is the lady for you. I have a meal with her occasionally and we compare notes. Now we'll have you to discuss.' She gave him a cheeky grin. 'I reckon you'll like Sarah.'

'The important thing is whether Chief likes *her*. He's a very discriminating dog where humans are concerned.'

Baxter watched as the German Shepherd nuzzled Julie's hand while staring up at her with adoration in his big dark eyes. Then Julie ruffled the thick hair around his neck and he made a soft sound of contentment.

'You're a lovely dog,' she told Chief. 'Just the kind of dog every Greg Baxter should have, except that there is only one Greg Baxter.' She shot Baxter a grin and brushed dog hair from her slacks as she stood up. 'See you again before too long—and I'll bring some bait with me.'

•

'Ah, well, Chief,' Baxter said, when Julie had left, 'we'd better go to the vet. She'll give you a needle in the neck, which you won't like, but I don't want to lose you.'

He couldn't be sure, but it seemed the German Shepherd's whole body drooped at the mention of the word 'vet'.

Two blessedly uneventful days passed before Baxter drove a reluctant Chief to his appointment. Sarah Morrison was indeed a lovely young woman, and she handled the dog with great care and professionalism. But Chief clearly wasn't on quite the same high as he'd been around Julie. Neither was Baxter.

'That's a great spot by the river you've got there, Mr Baxter,' Sarah said with a friendly smile. 'I was over there a couple of times. Old Harry gave me a flathead once.' Her lips quirked. 'Julie told me you cooked her a great fish lunch.'

What *hadn't* Julie told her, Baxter wondered.

'Yes, it's a terrific spot,' he said. 'Too good really. It lures one away from the desk.' He hooked Chief's leash on—the dog was still casting him black looks of betrayal—and led him to the door. 'I'd better push off. Nice to have met you, Dr Morrison.'

'I hope you'll call me Sarah the next time we meet,' she said, and smiled in a way that let him know she was interested in seeing more of him.

'And I'm Greg,' he said, smiling too. But he didn't ask her out for a coffee.

•

Later that day, sitting on his verandah, Baxter reviewed the positives of the past week, trying to keep the negatives at bay.

His circle of Moondilla acquaintances had increased by three—two of them female. His mother would be over the moon if he told her that he'd met up with Julie again. Not to mention a young female vet who might be interested in him.

But while entertaining Sarah would be pleasant, it wasn't the ideal route to book authorship. Women could be relied upon to waylay one's best intentions. Besides, they weren't allowed for in his budget. Sarah was more affluent than him, and she wouldn't expect him to be a cheapskate.

Of course, his mother didn't understand his reluctance to start a relationship. Though she'd written half a dozen books, they were cookbooks. She simply compiled a whack of recipes and then employed a top photographer. The formula was the same whether the recipes originated in Australia, Asia or anywhere else.

A novel was an entirely different proposition. A novel was tough. A great many people wrote novels, but only a fraction were actually published. It was a long, hard grind, and Baxter couldn't afford to mess around with women. Well, unless she was a very special woman, one who stood out.

He decided to think about something else.

His mind drifted to the drug problem. The only good side was that a drug bust in Moondilla could form the basis for another book. There was this fellow Franco Campanelli, who sounded like a creep if ever there was a creep—he'd make a colourful character. The Mr Big of the drug scene. Baxter didn't want to just write about him, though. He wanted to take him on.

CHAPTER NINE

In the expectation that he'd at least have Julie Rankin to entertain, Baxter decided he needed some extra refreshments. Although reluctant to spend a lot of money, he thought he should pick up some wine, in case Julie preferred it to orange juice. The Family Hotel stocked a decent selection. So Baxter drove into town one Saturday morning, bought his groceries and then went to the hotel.

On his passage through the back saloon, his eyes lit upon a very attractive blonde woman, probably in her early thirties. She appeared to have a lot of class: she certainly stood out from everyone else in the hotel. He paused, watching her. She was, next to Julie Rankin, the most stand-out woman he'd seen in Moondilla.

She was in the company of a dark-haired man who might have been a good stamp of a fellow in his younger days. But he'd clearly imbibed more booze than was good for him; his face was flushed and a very loud argument was in progress. The blonde woman wanted to leave the hotel and her bloke didn't.

'Ya not going, ya bitch,' he said heatedly, grabbing her by the arm. 'I know why you want to leave. That Eytie bastard is back and he wants you to run one of his dirty parties.'

'Don't be stupid, Jack.'

'Don't call *me* stupid, ya stupid bitch!'

Jack . . . Jack Drew? Baxter wondered. It seemed almost certain, meaning the woman was probably his wife, Liz.

She was struggling to pull away from him. 'I can't stand Campanelli,' she hissed, 'so you needn't think I'd have anything to do with him, let alone go out on his yacht.'

'More lies, Liz!' Drew roared.

'You've had too much to drink, and I'm not staying here to be insulted.'

'You bloody well *are* staying if I say so.' And with that he gave her a backhander across one cheek.

It must have carried a fair amount of force because Liz stumbled and almost fell at Baxter's feet. He stooped to help her up, before sitting her down at an adjacent table. She was clutching her face and sobbing.

There were several people, mostly male, drinking in the saloon as well as at the bar, but not one of them—not even the big bartender—moved to intercede on Liz's behalf. Baxter glanced around at them and shook his head in disbelief.

He walked back to where Drew was standing and looked him up and down. 'That was a gutless, mongrel thing to do. What kind of a man are you to hit a woman?'

Drew's face flushed a deeper red as his sodden brain registered these remarks. There was absolute silence in the saloon, and Baxter realised that the other drinkers—those gutless bastards—were waiting for the fireworks to begin. Drunk or sober, Jack Drew had probably ruled the roost around here for years.

'Who the hell do you think you are?' the boozy ex-pug shouted.

'A fellow who thinks that any man who hits a woman is a low creep and a complete mongrel. Not a man at all, just a grub,' Baxter said coolly.

'Interferin' bastard. *I'll* give you interference.' Drew rolled up his sleeves. 'You want to step outside?'

Baxter laughed in his face. 'You couldn't walk that far. You're too drunk to walk straight, let alone fight.'

'I'll give you *walk*,' Drew said, swaying closer to Baxter.

Drunk though he was, Drew still knew how to throw a punch. It was obviously second nature to him, and a hook can do a lot of damage. If delivered properly, it can break a man's jaw, not to mention put him to sleep.

Baxter harnessed the momentum of the hook with a sharp blow to Drew's extended arm, turning the ex-pug halfway around. Then Baxter delivered two massive hits, leaving Drew out cold on the carpet.

A collective gasp rose up from the room as Baxter straightened his clothes.

Liz was still stooped on the chair, her face swelling. The bartender had at least handed her some ice wrapped in a tea towel.

Baxter crouched down in front of her. 'You want to get out of here?'

She nodded, then smiled as best she could. Tears were streaming down her face, so he handed her a wad of napkins from the bar. Once she'd dried her eyes, he held his arm out for her to take and steered her outside. 'Your husband won't be in a fit state to drive you anywhere for quite a while,' he said. 'I can take you home.'

'That's very sweet of you, but I'm fine. Our car's just over there.'

She started walking across the hotel courtyard and he stayed by her side. He honestly didn't think she was up to driving—her right eye was swollen shut, and at the very least she'd be pretty uncomfortable without the ice she was pressing to her face.

'I'll be happier to know you're home safely,' he said.

But Liz's attention was suddenly elsewhere. 'Oh, Christ,' she muttered.

He glanced around. 'What's the problem?'

'It's coming towards us. That big fellow and his sidekick.'

'HEY *YOU*,' a huge voice boomed across the hotel court-yard. 'What are you doing with that woman?'

'Keep walking,' Baxter said softly. 'Take no notice of him. Is it Campanelli?'

'Yes, that's Campanelli.' Liz was shaking.

Baxter opened the car door for her, and then turned around and took in the two men behind him. Campanelli was very stout with a slightly reddish complexion; he looked like an Italian tenor beginning to put on weight. He was dressed in an ill-fitting but expensive suit. His companion was a thickset thug with ginger hair and mean eyes.

'Are you a relation of this lady?' Baxter asked Campanelli.

'No, but what are you doing with her?' the man retorted arrogantly.

'It's none of your business what I'm doing with her, but as she and her husband aren't in a fit state to drive, I'm taking the lady home. That satisfy you?'

'The hell it does.'

Baxter straightened to his full height and glared down at Campanelli. 'I've answered your question and my advice is for you to waddle off home, Fatso. If you stay here, you'll find yourself in a heap of trouble.'

'Skeeter,' Campanelli said harshly, looking at his goon, 'feed this clown a knuckle sandwich.'

Skeeter rushed forward and threw a roundhouse punch that missed Baxter by a metre or so. As the goon prepared to throw another, Baxter gave him a terrific blow that virtually lifted him off his feet, then dumped him on the ground.

'Are you hard of hearing, Campanelli?' Baxter asked calmly. 'I told you to waddle off home. You've got no business here.'

Wide-eyed, Campanelli looked at his man on the ground. Then he lunged at Baxter. Keeping his cool, Baxter stepped to one side, slapping Campanelli on one side of the face, then the other—very substantial slaps that flipped the big man around.

'Get going, Fatso,' Baxter said, and kicked him in the backside.

This threw Campanelli off balance, and he fell facedown on the ground.

By now everyone from the bar was crowded outside the hotel, watching and whispering—and sniggering. Campanelli's face flushed beetroot red. The whole town would soon know that he'd been made to look ineffective.

'By Christ, I'll get you, you bastard,' he muttered under his breath, so that only Baxter could hear, as he got up and staggered towards his shiny blue Mercedes. He slid in and backed out of the courtyard without showing a skerrick of concern for Skeeter.

As the Mercedes sped off, a white police car skidded to a stop in the courtyard. A tall, middle-aged officer got out and came across to where Baxter was standing over the fallen thug.

'What's going on here?' the officer asked. 'Why was Mr Campanelli on the ground? And that other man, what's wrong with him?'

Baxter looked the policeman up and down before answering.
'Who are you? Just so I know who I'm talking to.'

'Sergeant Ron Cross.' He held up his identification.

CHAPTER TEN

Alarm bells rang in Baxter's head.

'And your name, sir?' Cross asked, his blue eyes cold and hard.

'Greg Baxter.'

Cross took out a notepad and pen, writing it down. 'Well, Mr Baxter, you can either explain yourself here or down at the station.'

Baxter called out to Liz, who was sitting in the car with the door open. 'Excuse me, Mrs Drew? This officer needs to talk to both of us.'

'No worries,' Liz called back, and gestured for the two men to walk over.

She gave Cross a wary half-smile as he nodded a curt greeting and asked for her statement. Once she'd laid out the facts, an amused twinkle appeared in her good eye. 'This man also kicked Mr Campanelli in the backside, Sergeant.'

'I see,' Cross said, staring at Baxter with respect, but also a challenge. 'Do you have anything to add?'

When Baxter shook his head, Cross asked how he could be contacted. Baxter provided his phone number and said, 'I'm out at the old Carpenter place, working away at a novel, so you can reach me there pretty much anytime.'

If Cross was on the take, the whole drug ring would now be aware of exactly the kind of man who'd bought their coveted property. They weren't likely to approach Baxter now—well, not in a friendly way.

•

As he pulled his car out of the courtyard, Baxter smiled across at Liz Drew. 'Well, now, the fat is well and truly in the fire. And by the way, I'm Greg Baxter.'

'Liz Drew,' she said. 'But you seem to know that already.'

'I've heard a lot about you.'

'What have you heard, Mr Baxter?'

'Greg, please. What have I heard?' He didn't want to bring up Jack. 'Mostly that you're a great-looking woman. But they haven't done you justice.'

She smiled and winced, pressing the half-melted ice against her face.

They were driving down Moondilla's main street. 'Where do I take you?' Baxter asked, and she gave him some directions.

'It really is very sweet of you to go to this bother,' she added.

'It's no bother. None at all.'

'I meant intervening with Jack.'

'That was no bother either,' Baxter said, and then couldn't help asking, 'How did you get mixed up with a boozy husband like that?'

'It's too long a story to tell now.'

He'd thought she might say that. 'That's fine. Ah, here we are.' He pulled up outside a well-presented timber home.

'Would you like to come in for lunch or a cup of coffee?' Liz asked.

'No thanks, I've got to get back to my writing.' The truth was, he didn't feel comfortable being alone with a married woman in her house, even though her husband was a creep. Baxter had very strict rules about that sort of thing. He also didn't want Liz to act the hostess when she needed some peace.

'Fair enough.' Liz started to get out of the car, then turned back to him. She seemed flustered. 'Look, again, thanks very much for taking my part. Nobody in town has ever opposed Jack.' She paused, frowning. 'Well, that's not exactly true. Jack and Campanelli had a big fight once.'

'What about?'

'Me. Campanelli's always been crooked on me marrying Jack. He wanted me when I was with the country and western troupe—he came to all of our shows.'

Baxter raised a querying eyebrow.

'I used to sing,' she explained, a sad and faraway look in her eyes that reminded him of Julie. 'Anyway, Campanelli wouldn't have married me. He wanted me for . . . well, other reasons.' She seemed very uncomfortable.

'You don't have to explain anything.'

'I feel I do,' she said.

'Not today, anyway. You should rest.' Baxter grinned reassuringly. 'The other thing is, I've got a big dog I left at home, Chief. He'll be getting worried about me.'

Liz laughed. 'That's the first time I've heard that excuse. He must be some dog. What kind is he?'

'A German Shepherd bred from imported stock.'

'Ah, I love that breed. We had mostly kelpie and cattle dog cross at home in Queensland. We needed them for the herd.'

It sounded like she was an Outback girl, raised on a station. 'I should think a cattle dog would be a very handy acquisition. Keep the likes of Campanelli in line,' Baxter said and smiled.

Liz smiled too. 'I'm very pleased to have met you, Greg. In fact, I'd say you're the most interesting man I've ever met in Moondilla. And that includes my husband.'

'Thanks,' Baxter said, 'but I'm also sorry to hear that.'

'Well.' Liz sighed. 'Jack's not bad when he's not drinking. He helps keep the place tidy and all. The problem is, it's not too often these days that he *isn't* drinking.' She dabbed at her sore face, checking the damage in the car mirror. 'I'd be much happier if he just went off and fished. He's got a little boat and he's a good mechanic. Maybe not as good as Steve

Lewis, but good enough. He can fix just about anything, from lawnmowers to council bulldozers. Why he's on the grog beats me. But that's men for you.'

Baxter shook his head firmly. 'I don't know the first thing about engines, but I don't drink. When you're ranked as high as I am in martial arts, you're supposed to lead an exemplary life. That's according to Eastern teaching. Can't say I do it perfectly—it's hard in Western society—but I do my best. No smoking, no drinking and no junk food.'

Liz grinned as she got out of the car. 'You sound too good to be true.'

CHAPTER ELEVEN

Back at home, Baxter was preoccupied with the layout of his book—principally, how to end it. He'd come across many otherwise good books that ended very poorly, so he was putting a lot of effort into concluding the book he'd come to think of as *River of Dreams.*

He'd already decided, after weeks of thought, that he should begin the book with the story of Rosa. This had started out as a piece of investigative journalism, one of the most popular he'd ever written. Baxter had titled it 'Fallen Angel'. With some expansion and embellishment, and with names and details changed, he thought it couldn't be bettered for the opening chapter.

He was hard at work when the phone rang. It was Julie

Rankin, and she proposed coming out for a quick lunch and maybe a fish.

Well, that was what she told him. Once she arrived, it was soon apparent that what she really wanted was his account of the brouhaha at the Family Hotel.

'What on earth induced you to take on Campanelli?' she asked, after taking a sip of white wine and declaring it excellent. Baxter had made a second trip to pick some up, and now he was glad of it.

The answer to her question was straightforward enough. 'He's a bully and I hate bullies,' Baxter said. 'And besides, I had to defend myself. He's a creep, Julie.'

'Granted he's a creep, but he's an important creep in Moondilla.' She was smiling, but her eyes were troubled. 'He could make things tough for you.'

'I'll watch my back.'

The thought of Campanelli 'getting' him seemed ludicrous, but there was truth to what Julie said—the man had resources. Of course, Baxter wouldn't tell her what Campanelli had muttered before getting in his Mercedes. It would only worry her.

A change of subject was in order. 'Do you mind bringing your wine outside?' he asked. 'I've got something I want to show you.' They headed onto the verandah, where Chief was snoozing in the sun. 'I've been working on the layout of my novel,' Baxter explained, gesturing to the stack of pages. 'Do you have time to read the first chapter?'

She grinned and stared down at the pages, and Baxter was pleased to see that she seemed fascinated. 'It's my day off. Not that it means anything—I'm on call just about all the time. But I'd love to take a peek.'

'Thanks,' Baxter said, handing 'Fallen Angel' to her. 'I'll go on making notes while you read it.'

When she'd finished, Julie looked at Baxter and nodded. 'It's very good. Sad, but good. If a girl decides she wants to make a living via prostitution, that's one thing, but having to live that way to fund a drug habit is another matter.'

'Thanks, Julie. That's exactly what I set out to say.'

'And this is how you're going to start your book?'

'That's the plan. I reckon it puts the whole rotten drug business into focus.'

'It does.' The troubled look was in her eyes again.

'You know,' Baxter said, 'I came back here because I needed to get away to a different kind of lifestyle. Finding out about the drugs . . . well, it's really taken the gilt off the gingerbread.'

'Yes, I felt the same way when I realised how bad it was.'

'Let's hope that Latham and Company can clean it up, and then Moondilla will revert to what it was.' He sighed. 'Or maybe that's wishful thinking.'

'It's still a nice place,' Julie said. 'A bit dull for some people, but—drugs aside, of course—you don't come down here if you're looking for excitement. You come to fish and to smell the flowers and to enjoy the river and the ocean.'

She looked as though she loved it as much as he did, and he realised her words echoed Mr Garland's from so long ago.

'That's right,' he said vehemently, the thought of the old fisherman stirring his anger, 'and it's obscene for Moondilla to be fouled up by drugs. I'll do everything I can to help Latham and his team clean it up.'

'Very laudable,' she said, nodding. 'I feel the same way. But let's be cautious—we won't be any help if we put ourselves in danger.'

Baxter nodded, although he knew it was a bit late for that.

Julie had finished her wine. 'What a relief that I haven't been called in to work,' she said. 'If you can spare the time, I'd like to introduce you to some of my family—my sister Jane and her husband Steve, the fishing fanatic.'

'Good idea. I'd love to meet them, and I could ask Steve to tune up Flora.'

'Flora?'

'My runabout—you know, the *Flora Jane*.'

•

So Baxter spent a lovely afternoon with Julie and the Lewises.

Jane was a nice-looking woman—not as classically good-looking as Julie, but very attractive and with a great personality. Sherrie was a stunning seventeen-year-old who did indeed look like a young Julie, while Jason was fifteen, a solid boy whose main interest appeared to be sailing sabots on the river.

Baxter soon heard from the horse's mouth that Jason wasn't very good at cricket or football, so he wasn't in the upper echelon of boys at the high school. Conversely, Sherrie was an excellent tennis player and swimmer, and Jason thought it extremely unfair that his sister was so good at sport, especially because she didn't take it seriously.

In Steve Lewis, Baxter thought he'd found a true friend. Lewis was a lean fellow, quite nice-looking, with dark hair and keen grey eyes. He'd taken over Moondilla Motors after serving his apprenticeship there with his dad. Now in his late thirties, Lewis was recognised as one of the best mechanics on the South Coast, and had the Holden Agency in Moondilla. Jane had gotten to know Steve while working in the garage's office, and it was clear there'd never been anyone else for either of them.

The two men got on like a house on fire, and were soon talking fishing. Lewis was one of the keenest fishermen ever to tie on a hook. Needless to say, he had his own boat, a bigger and more modern craft than Baxter's. As Julie had implied, he was occasionally accused by his wife of being *too* keen, but Baxter's plea for a boat tune-up seemed to fall on fertile ground. From the look in Jane's eye and her encouragement of the idea, Baxter guessed that she'd soon be pushing her husband for more info about him.

'So what have you got in mind once I've looked at your *Flora Jane*?' Lewis asked.

'Well, I've never gone out past the river mouth because I'm an inexperienced sailor, and I don't know the best fishing spots anyway. So I'd appreciate having someone with me who knows the ropes.'

'We've got a couple of busy weekends coming up, so how about I come by on Saturday arvo in a few weeks?' Lewis suggested. 'I'll work on the boat then and we'll take her out for a bit. Another time, weather willing, we'll make an early start and duck out to the Islands before the wind gets up. You can fish from out in front of them if the nor'easter isn't blowing—if it is, and there's a run-in tide, you can get thrown up against the rocks. It's a dicey place at the best of times, but the fishing is great, with lots of snapper on offer. You just need to know what you're about.'

'Sounds terrific.'

'Have you got plenty of gear?'

'Probably not as much as I should have. I've got a couple of rods and reels, and half a dozen handlines, but no lures. I don't understand how to use them.'

'Not to worry. You've been catching fish, haven't you?'

'Some, though not a lot. Of course there's only me and an occasional visitor—Julie appreciated my fillet.' He shot her a smile, which she returned. 'But the thing is that my mother's due to visit soon, and she's a big-time chef and cooking writer.'

'You don't mean Frances Baxter, the Great Woman?' Jane asked, astonished.

'That's her,' Baxter said and grinned, while Jane shot Julie an annoyed glance for not keeping her in the loop. 'So I'd like to have some decent fish on hand.'

CHAPTER TWELVE

The next week passed without incident. Then, late one morning, Chief's bark warned Baxter that he could expect a visitor. The dog stood at attention in the doorway of the shed where his master had been working out.

'Let him be, Chief,' Baxter said when he saw it was Drew.

The German Shepherd moved to sit beside him, hackles still raised, while the ex-pug sauntered into the shed.

'Can I help you?' Baxter asked, cool and steady.

'You're the bastard who hit me while I was drunk,' Drew snarled.

'As I remember, you tried to hit me before I touched you.'

'You were lucky. I don't give a shit for your fancy martial arts.' Drew walked right up to Baxter and tried to stare him down.

Baxter looked Drew over, making it clear that he didn't think much of what he saw. 'You're a gutless, worthless bloke, Drew. No worthwhile man hits his wife. She's a decent woman too, and I can't imagine why she'd have taken you on. She ought to dump you and go back to Queensland.'

'Think you know a lot, don't you?' Drew sneered.

'I only know what I've been told. I've talked to people, and it seems you're in the habit of hitting Liz,' Baxter said, letting contempt drip from his voice. 'Go home, Drew. Go home while you can. You're a boozer and a has-been.'

Drew flushed red and leaned even closer. 'I'll give you has-been. I'm going to see how much ticker you've got. I fought some of the best men in the game—real fighters, they were, not fancy martial arts fellas.'

'A fat lot of good it did you. What have you got to show for it? The best thing you've got is your wife, and you belt her.'

'You'll be sorry you said that. I'll put *you* in hospital this time.'

Chief growled, standing to attention again, and Drew laughed.

'Or are you a bloody coward who's going to set your dog on me?'

'Outside, Chief,' said Baxter sharply, and the dog obeyed in an instant. Then Baxter turned back to Drew. 'Listen, go home to your grog. I wouldn't waste my time on a fellow like you. I'm getting back to my training.' Baxter just wanted this to be over with as quickly as possible. He turned his back on the ex-pug.

As he'd expected, this show of contempt ignited Drew, who obviously had a low boiling point. He stepped around Baxter and poked a hard straight left at him. He probably reckoned that if Baxter put up his hands to counter, he'd give him a hard rip in the breadbasket to soften him up. That move might have taken down a boxer, even a great one, but Baxter saw it all coming.

While Drew had likely faced some fast men, Baxter knew he'd never been in the ring with a fellow who moved as fast as him. He didn't throw up his hands to ward off the straight left. Instead, he spun around, hitting Drew with three hammer blows in quick succession—one took the ex-pug under the chin and lifted him off the ground. He would have been blacking out when the third blow struck.

Baxter looked down at the prostrate figure at his feet. 'Bloody idiot,' he muttered.

•

Once he'd arranged Drew in the most comfortable position possible and given him some first aid, Baxter headed back to the house. Chief followed him in.

First Baxter arranged an ambulance, then he perused the local phone book and rang Mrs Drew. 'Liz, I've got some bad news. I've just called the ambos to come out here and pick up your husband. He'll probably need a night or two in hospital.'

'So he had another go,' Liz said with a sigh.

'Afraid so. He was sober this time.'

'Did he touch you, Greg?'

'He didn't even get close, Liz.'

'Ah.' She didn't sound surprised. 'Well, Julie and I warned him not to go near you. Maybe he'll stay away now.'

'I should say he will.' Before they said goodbye, Baxter added, 'You'd better wangle a trip out here with Julie so you can pick up your car.'

He couldn't do anything more for Drew, so he took a quick shower and settled himself at his desk, planning to read his previous day's writing. Then the phone rang.

'You all right, Greg?' Julie asked, skipping the pleasantries. Once he'd reassured her, she said, 'I warned Jack not to go near you.'

'Well, when you've got Drew in the clinic, you tell him that if I hear he's hit his wife again, I'll chew him up properly. Liz seems a really nice woman—how the blazes did she get tangled up with that creep?'

'I might tell you the story sometime.'

Soon enough the ambulance arrived. The two ambos, one male and one female, had clearly been briefed by Julie. Once he'd greeted them, Baxter pointed towards the shed. 'He's in there.' He followed after them in case he could help. Drew was still out to it, and in a few minutes he was laid on a stretcher and placed in the ambulance.

'This is a new position for Jack,' the male ambo said, with a quirk of his lips.

'You could say it was his moment of truth,' Baxter said. 'He had an inflated view of his ability and belittled something he knew nothing about.'

•

As he recovered over the next several weeks, it became clear that Jack Drew had stopped hitting his wife. He also cut down on the booze and avoided getting in fights. Drew's fellow council workers couldn't get over the change in their workmate. He was fishing again. And then, to top it all off, he started doing up a gorgeous old car for Liz.

She rang Baxter and explained all of this, then thanked him for half-killing her husband. 'Jack had to be thoroughly beaten before he woke to the fact that he's not a super fighter. He thought he was top dog here and now he knows he isn't.'

Baxter smiled and shook his head as he put down the phone. Who needed to think up plots for novels when real-life stories abounded?

CHAPTER THIRTEEN

While Drew was getting himself back in order, Steve Lewis came to be Greg Baxter's fishing mate. Julie had been fishing with Baxter too—on the terms they'd negotiated—and they got along well, but Baxter just couldn't think of her as another bloke.

The two men, meanwhile, had developed an instant rapport and respect for the other's skills. Baxter knew very little about mechanics and was in awe of Steve's expertise in this field, on top of his talent for fishing. He guessed that Lewis admired his physique and the fact he was a martial arts champion.

On that first Saturday arvo, Lewis spent an hour or so on Baxter's boat and had her running very sweetly when he'd finished. The two men and Chief took *Flora* for a short run upriver, and then headed back against the tide. Baxter was driving and steering, with Lewis lending a hand when needed.

'Do you always take Chief out with you?' Lewis asked. His eyes were on the dog, who was clearly enjoying himself with the wind ruffling his thick fur.

'He'd be offended if I didn't,' Baxter said and grinned. 'Any problem?'

'Aw, no. He's pretty well behaved, isn't he?'

'Better than a child. He doesn't like other boats coming too close, but I'm getting him to understand that they're okay.'

'Julie says there's not a thing he doesn't know,' Lewis said. 'It's just that it can get a bit rough out at the Islands and he might fall overboard.'

'I doubt that he would, Steve. He stays in the cabin while I'm fishing.'

Lewis reached out to give Chief a pat, and the dog nuzzled his hand. To Baxter, this proved beyond a shadow of a doubt that Lewis was a true blue bloke.

'When I was a kid,' Lewis said, giving Chief's ears a scratch, 'the big fellows on the land all had a down on German Shepherds. They called them Alsatians in those days, and reckoned they had wolf in them. Their idea was that they might cross with dingoes and breed dogs that could pull down a beast, so the males all had to be castrated. Bloody stupid really—most farmers are their own worst enemies. A lot of them never tie up their dogs at night, and any of them could've mated with dingoes.'

Baxter nodded. 'I read up on how things used to be when I was trying to decide what breed of dog would suit me best. Back in those days, only the police and the services could import German Shepherds, but whenever a kid got lost the police would be called on to search with their shepherds! And the import ban did a lot of harm, because the Aussie dogs were becoming too closely bred and too highly strung.'

'Good thing they woke up and allowed imports again.'

'Too right. I'm convinced there's no breed more straight-out intelligent.'

Chief looked up at the two men, giving them a doggy grin, and they laughed.

•

When they came back to shore, Lewis declared *Flora* sound, and said he was relieved. 'Old Harry didn't use her very often, Greg,' he explained. 'His missus didn't like him taking her out on his own, and she used to get sick every time she stepped on a boat, so he mostly fished from the jetty or from the boat kellicked off the bank.'

They adjourned to the front verandah, where Baxter gave Lewis a beer while he had orange juice. Lewis eyed Baxter's drink with some amusement, and said he was only used to drinking with blokes who drank beer. 'You don't drink, Greg?'

'Don't drink and don't smoke and never did. It's part and parcel of the martial arts credo, especially when you get to my level. It's like you're a priest, as everyone looks up to the top black belts. But it's never worried me, so don't let it worry you, Steve.'

Lewis took this in good part. 'It doesn't worry me, Greg. It's just that I'm used to blokes drinking beer—but of course, none of them are black belts.'

'You've got to discipline yourself early on, and after a while the non-drinking becomes part of your way of life. A fellow can do anything if he really wants to. It's all in yourself.'

'I reckon it is,' Lewis agreed, but he added that he wasn't going to give up his beer: he wasn't a big drinker, but he liked a couple of beers at the end of the day.

●

They yarned well into the evening. Lewis knew everyone and Baxter was getting plenty of interesting information from him.

'And how are you getting on with my sister-in-law?' Lewis asked, after a brief break in their conversation.

'It depends on what you mean by "getting on",' Baxter said.

Lewis shook his head and took a sip of his beer. 'Damned funny woman, Julie. Never had a boyfriend. The best-looking girl in the district, but she never seemed interested in boys. Not girls, either, in case you're wondering.'

Baxter shrugged. 'I reckon Julie comes out here for a break, and maybe she's still missing her father. I cook her a meal and sometimes we have an hour or so fishing. She made it very plain that she wasn't looking for a relationship, and I respect that.' He just wished he could fully accept it.

'Julie's a nice person and a helluva good doctor—surgeon too, probably the best in the district—and she's been great with our kids. But she's just as happy to be out fishing as doing anything else. Those baggy jeans or shorts and a man's shirt she gets around in—from a distance you'd swear blind she was a bloke. And talk about tie hooks. Julie can tie a hook while I'm thinking about it.'

'I know what you mean,' Baxter said, grinning. 'I've seen her in action.'

'It must be a bit hard on you, Greg. What I mean is that Julie's a very attractive woman, but from all accounts she freezes right up if a bloke tries to get too close.'

Baxter considered this. Steve Lewis wasn't a dill—he thought things through, and he'd obviously thought about Julie Rankin over the years. And of course, he'd be privy to some privileged information about his sister-in-law.

'Do you know why Julie's like that, Steve?' Baxter asked. 'Since I met her, I've been trying to figure out if something made her that way, or whether she was always like that with blokes.'

'I've wondered too, but there's not one incident that stands out, and I've known her since I started seeing Jane, when Julie was still in high school. What was she like when she was living in Sydney, taking your class?'

Baxter told Lewis all about Julie's demeanour back then. 'And she actually *was* better than some of the men I taught. I kid you not, Steve. Not many women have the muscle power of men, but technique can make up for some of that, and that's where Julie shone. She could have clobbered quite a lot of men very easily.'

'Is that a fact.' Lewis looked impressed. 'I did hear she put a bloke in a hammer lock a few months ago, and took away his knife—he'd lost the plot at Bega Hospital. But I reckoned he must've been a weakling.'

'Well, he may have been. Whether she performs the old routines or even remembers them, I can't tell you. She watches me do mine and never joins in. She wants to give people the impression she's no pussycat, but I'm inclined to think she might have let the martial arts side of things slip because of her hands.'

Lewis nodded his understanding. 'I get you. Surgery's still her top priority.'

The conversation drifted away from Julie, and Baxter brought Lewis another beer and poured himself another juice. He hesitated before asking the question that had been in the back of his mind ever since Lewis arrived.

'Have you ever had anything to do with Franco Campanelli?'

Lewis gave Baxter a sharp look. 'Why do you ask?'

CHAPTER FOURTEEN

Baxter made an effort to sound casual. 'Well, you might have heard I had a bit of trouble with the big bloke—it was the same day I decked Jack Drew at the Family Hotel.'

Lewis burst out laughing and had to take a moment to calm down, have a sip of his beer and wipe his eyes. 'Yeah, everyone in town was talking about how you kicked his fat behind and sent him scurrying for his Mercedes. *That* I would like to have seen.'

'Sounds like you don't have much time for the man.'

'Well, I've done some work for him—he's got the Merc, two trawlers and a fancy yacht. He always pays on time, but he's not my cup of tea, to put it mildly.'

'Why's that?'

TONY PARSONS

'A lot of reasons. There's the fact he's got too much hoot for a trawler owner. They don't make that kind of money, not even with two trawlers. He gives flash parties, some out on his yacht, and there's always heaps of girls.'

That reminded Baxter of something, and he searched his memory—it was the argument between the Drews, weeks ago at the hotel. Drew had accused his wife of being involved with Campanelli's 'dirty parties'.

Lewis lowered his voice. 'There are rumours galore. The story is that Campanelli owns a brothel in Sydney and uses some of his girls to "entertain" his guests.'

Baxter scowled. 'It wouldn't surprise me.' He thought of the undercover policewoman who'd had to go 'all the way as a prostitute', in Latham's words.

'Look,' Lewis said, 'Julie wouldn't like me telling you this, but I reckon you should know. Campanelli tried to get her to go out on his yacht, but she wouldn't come at that.'

This made Baxter straighten, his fists clenching. 'Really?' He felt ready to throw all caution to the wind—swim out to that gaudy yacht, and pummel the creep into a pulp. He called on his training and tried to calm down. 'Did he threaten her?'

'No, fortunately. He thinks a lot of Julie—she operated on him for a burst appendix. She's one woman he won't bother too much. But she's aware that he's a heavy crumpet man, and you know, Julie hates the thought of women being exploited by men.'

'There's much more to Moondilla than appears on the surface,' Baxter said thoughtfully, wondering just how much Lewis knew, or had guessed.

'You can say that again. Did you know Campanelli once put the hard word on Liz Drew? That was before she married Jack.'

'She mentioned something about that when I was driving her home from the hotel. What's the full story?'

'Campanelli had the hots for Liz, Jack wanted her too, so they had a stoush. Campanelli can't fight, as you know all too well, but he's supposed to be able to wrestle and he's a strong bugger. Anyway, they had a go—not in public like the two of you—and apparently Drew cut him up pretty badly. The big fellow was heard to say he'd "get" Drew. That was a couple of years ago, but Drew is still here.'

So Baxter wasn't the only man who'd been threatened by a humiliated Campanelli. The fact that Drew was still alive and kicking was pretty reassuring—it seemed like an empty threat, and Baxter felt silly for paying it any mind.

'There's something very fishy about Campanelli,' Lewis said, 'and it isn't what swims about in the sea. I reckon I know what he's into, and that's drugs.'

Baxter raised his eyebrows. He trusted Lewis, but he didn't want to say anything because he'd given his word to Latham that he'd keep quiet.

'Yeah, that's what I reckon all right,' Lewis confirmed, 'but a fellow can't say it too loud or he might end up like that bloke in Griffith. There's been some queer things happen here lately. Blokes poking about that I don't know—and I know just about everyone in Moondilla. Man and boy I know them.'

'What kind of blokes?' Baxter asked.

'I reckon some are undercover coppers,' Lewis said. 'Then there's bad-looking fellows too. Could be crims because they sure look that way.'

'And I came back here because I thought Moondilla would be a nice, quiet place.'

'Nowhere's perfect, Greg.' Lewis's smile was thin. 'I reckon there's drugs coming in and I reckon this drug mob picked Moondilla because it was such a nice, quiet place—they thought nobody would trouble them. Then there's the trawlers that can meet incoming boats and land the drugs on shore. I hear things and what I hear I don't like.'

Baxter sipped the last of his orange juice and looked down the river. If you believed what was in the Bible, even Eden had its share of problems. Lewis was right, there was no perfect place. There were always those who weren't fussy about how they made money. It didn't matter how much grief they caused or how many people died.

'Sorry for troubling you, Greg,' Lewis said, his voice tinged with regret. 'I'm spoiling your view of the town, and you just moved back here recently.'

If only Lewis could know the whole story, Baxter thought. He gave his mate a reassuring smile. 'No worries, I like to know the score. And I really can't say if I'll stay here that long. I still love this place, but I've only got so much money put by, and if my first book doesn't succeed I'll probably have to go back to Sydney.'

'I hear you're a pretty good cook. Worked for your mother, didn't you?'

'From time to time. It's come in handy, but I'm not keen on it full-time.'

'The word is there's to be a new flash restaurant just outside Moondilla on the Sydney road. It's a great spot, overlooking the ocean. Could be the place for you.'

'Thanks Steve, that sounds all right. I don't want to take on a day job, but I'll probably need to—writing is a tough game. If you make it big, say on the international market, it can be very profitable, but the average Aussie author doesn't earn much.'

'I take off my hat to anyone who can write. I have trouble putting two sentences together, but give me an engine and I'm right at home.'

'I reckon I'm the opposite,' Baxter said, and the men exchanged grins.

'Well,' Lewis said, getting up, 'this place is tough to leave but I'd better make tracks. Jane told me not to be late for dinner. And that reminds me, she asked if you'd like to come round tomorrow night. Julie will be there—she gave Jane one of your recipes and they're trying it out.'

'I'll look forward to it, mate. And thanks for seeing to *Flora Jane*. Can't wait to take her for a spin to the Islands and stock up my freezer for Mum.'

CHAPTER FIFTEEN

The next day, Baxter called Jane to ask what he could contribute to the dinner, and she said he could bring one of his apple pies—the pastry was so light it threatened to blow away, was how Julie had described them to the Lewises. So Baxter baked one along with a smaller rhubarb pie, thinking that Sherrie and Jason would bypass the rhubarb in favour of the apple.

Jane had told him that there'd be a couple of others in attendance: a woman called Verna Graham—the receptionist at Julie's clinic—and her daughter Lisa, one of Sherrie's closest girlfriends at Moondilla High. Verna could have been described as a faded beauty, with darkened blonde hair streaked with grey, and some lines about her neck and eyes. Lisa was fresh-faced and pretty—not as lovely as Sherrie, but maybe Baxter was biased because of the Lewis girl's resemblance to Julie.

The evening began quite normally. Jane had made roast pork with a white wine gravy—Baxter's recipe, which she'd cooked to perfection. All except Baxter had wine with their meal, and he noticed that Verna topped up her glass more than the others. The pies went down well with dollops of vanilla ice-cream, and then everyone moved to the lounge room where the Lewises served coffee. The schoolgirls were allowed to stay up, while Jason headed off to bed.

'A very nice dinner, Jane,' Baxter said, sitting down in one of the big leather lounge chairs. 'You got it just right.'

'I'm so relieved—I was worried I'd mess it up. Oh, I almost forgot to mention,' Jane added, addressing herself to Verna Graham, 'that Greg is, or was, a professional chef with his mother. You'll have seen her on the telly.'

'Yes, I've heard about your mother being the Great Woman,' said Verna to Greg. 'Lisa's told me a lot about you.' There was a twinkle in her eyes, and her face was a little flushed from the wine. 'Evidently you've been a topic of discussion at Moondilla High. Isn't that so, Lisa?'

Her daughter blushed bright red. 'Well, er, he *has*, actually.' She looked as though she wanted to flee the room, but was too polite. Sherrie squirmed uncomfortably too.

Surprised, Baxter glanced between the girls. 'You must have little of interest to discuss if you're talking about me,' he said wryly.

'It seems,' Verna said, an amused eyebrow raised, 'that you're regarded as the town's resident hunk.'

'Good grief!' Baxter chuckled. 'I'm a bit too old to be called a hunk.'

'It's hard to imagine you as anything but young,' Verna said, and the girls nodded.

'Well, I guess I'll take the compliment as given,' he said. He smiled at Julie, who'd been following the conversation with close interest, and she grinned back.

'All we were discussing,' Sherrie put in, obviously trying to maintain some dignity, 'was the difference between Mr Baxter and Franco Campanelli.'

'The *difference*? I should say they're at opposite poles,' Verna said, her mouth tucking down at the corners. 'Franco Campanelli is a grub. He was born a grub, and an oversexed grub into the bargain.'

'Do you know much about him?' Baxter asked.

'I certainly do. You know, I haven't spoken about this in years—it's not pleasant—but he virtually ruined my life.'

Baxter caught significant looks from Steve Lewis and Julie.

'Do you want the girls to hear this, Verna?' Jane asked worriedly.

'It won't do them any harm to hear what Campanelli's like,' Lewis said, giving his wife's arm a reassuring squeeze. Sherrie nodded and sat forward eagerly in her chair.

'As for Lisa,' Verna said, 'he's already spoken to her about her working for him.'

'Mum!' Lisa exclaimed.

'Good heavens, *has* he?' Jane gasped, going white. 'A seven-teen-year-old schoolgirl?' Her gaze—and her husband's—moved to Sherrie. Baxter could see that as soon as they were in private, the family would be having a long chat.

'I'd prefer to see her dead,' Verna announced, while Lisa dropped her burning face into her hands and groaned. 'He's an awful man. Years ago, Bob and me borrowed money to buy the fish and chip shop. We were going all right, too—and then Campanelli got his father to build a rival place, big and flashy. They had the advantage of using their own fish, and could offer larger pieces than us, who had to buy everything.' She pulled out a hankie and dabbed at her eyes. 'So we had to let that slip.'

'Does Campanelli still own the shop?' Baxter asked. 'If so, I won't go near it.'

'Not anymore, but for a long time. After I lost Bob, he offered me a job there, subject to certain conditions that I won't spell out. I told him what he could do with the job. They were hard to come by, and God knows I needed one, but there was no way I was going to work for *him*.' She blew her nose and tucked her hankie away. 'Then the lovely Dr Rankin gave me a job as his receptionist and I was with him until the day he died. I'm still there, thanks to Julie.' Verna smiled at her boss.

There was a pause, and Lisa seized the opportunity to escape. 'Sherrie, I'd love to see that new dress you were telling me about,' she said, giving her friend a hopeful glance. The girls said a quick goodnight to the adults and hurried from the room.

'Sorry for bringing the mood down, everyone,' said Verna. 'I reckon I had a nip too much wine.' She'd finished her coffee and seemed to have sobered up.

'Sounds as though you've been on your own for some time,' Baxter said sympathetically. 'How did you lose your husband, if you don't mind me asking?'

Verna's eyes filled with tears again. 'He went out on a fishing trawler and didn't come back. The story—' she said derisively '—was that he fell overboard and drowned.'

'And you didn't believe it?' Baxter asked. He noticed Julie sitting up straighter.

'Listen, this isn't something I've told Lisa—it would just upset her—so please don't mention it to anyone outside this room.' They all nodded. 'Bob may have drowned,' Verna said, her voice almost at a whisper, 'but I reckon he had some help. He was found with a fractured skull. It supposedly happened when he fell overboard.'

'And you don't think it did?' Julie asked.

'I don't know for sure one way or another. I only know that Bob didn't come back, and not long after his death Campanelli put the hard word on me.'

Julie looked very concerned. 'I hope he's not still worrying you,' she said. 'You should tell me if he does.'

'Oh no, I'm yesterday's woman,' Verna replied and chuckled dryly. 'Campanelli isn't interested in old girls like me. He only likes young women. Schoolgirls, for preference. Look at the way he approached Lisa.'

Baxter glanced at Steve Lewis and shook his head. 'I didn't kick the creep hard enough when I had the opportunity,' he said, and Lewis nodded grimly.

The evening soon wound up, with Verna apologising profusely and everyone assuring her that it was a good thing to get a load off her chest.

As he drove home along the dark coastal roads, Baxter found himself deep in thought. He wasn't sure why, but he sensed that the time was approaching when he'd have to take on Campanelli once more. He hoped he was given the opportunity to fix the big mongrel good and proper. All this talk of young women being threatened and used by thugs was making him remember Rosa, and the story he'd called 'Fallen Angel'.

CHAPTER SIXTEEN

The girl was almost nineteen and she'd been a prostitute for nearly two years. She was a blonde, pretty girl with a good figure. Not so long ago she'd been much prettier, but the heroin had taken the edge off her looks. Her skin beneath the makeup now lacked bloom, and there were shadows under her eyes. Still, she attracted her share of the blokes who flocked to the Cross for sex.

The girl's name was Rosa. She'd once belonged to parents who loved her and who would never have envisaged her in her current surroundings. That was before Rosa's mother died and her father remarried. Rosa's stepmother didn't give her the love she'd received from her mum, but she did what she thought was best for Rosa. She was, in fact, overzealous in her concern for her stepdaughter's welfare, trying to put the brakes on Rosa seeing boys early in her teens. Rosa's father sided with his new wife, who was younger than him and attractive into the bargain.

The atmosphere in the Craig home became so oppressive and restrictive that the high-spirited Rosa decided she could stand it no longer. She'd discussed the situation with her best friend Prue, who was in an even worse situation: Prue had a drunken father who mauled her and brought women to the house.

Rosa and Prue decided they would go to Sydney, where they were sure it wouldn't be too difficult to obtain employment. They'd been told by other girls that it was relatively easy to find jobs as waitresses. Once they'd earned some money and could dress well, they reckoned they could hold their own with most girls their age.

And they were right—they didn't have much trouble finding jobs as waitresses at a swanky restaurant. They rented a flat and got a big kick out of togging themselves out in the latest fashions.

And then Rosa started chatting to Alan, one of her regular customers at the restaurant. He was a ruggedly handsome bloke who seemed to have lashings of money, yet didn't work. They had sex the second week, and it was Alan who introduced Rosa to heroin. Prue tried it too. When the opportunity arose, Alan had sex with her as well—by then, the girls cared more about the drug than him.

Rosa and Prue soon discovered that they needed more heroin than their wages could purchase. That was why they started taking men. At first there were only a few men in Alan's flat and then, as they needed more money for heroin, they had to take more. Alan told them they had to do whatever men asked of them, and do it well because there were plenty of other girls to compete with. Ideally, he said, they should be so good in bed that the same men would come to them on a regular basis.

The first week was the worst for both girls. But after they survived that, the numbers of men and the requests that had to be obeyed didn't seem to make much difference. Well, they *did*, but the heroin compensated for what the girls had to do.

It became a matter of trying to attract as many men as possible, because that gave them the money to give Alan for the heroin their bodies craved. He passed on some money to his supplier, kept a percentage for himself and amassed a tidy pool from his two girls. He'd had other girls, but they hadn't lasted as long. Rosa and Prue gave him free sex—and if they didn't give it to him satisfactorily, he would threaten to cut off their supply for a period. This brought them to heel and they would do anything he asked.

Alan had been the quasi-leader of a gang of street kids before he came to Kings Cross, and he'd built up a reputation as an enforcer. One of his earlier girls had died from an overdose, another had been knifed, and yet another—the only one of that trio who didn't use drugs—had mysteriously disappeared. The rumour was that Mavis had saved a lot of money from screwing and got out. If so, she was one of the few who was able to exit the game.

•

Greg Baxter had seen Rosa several times. Despite her tight, low-cut blouse and skimpy skirt, she reminded him very much of Elaine. She had the same look of gentility. Baxter resolved to meet her.

A few nights later, Baxter was across the road from Rosa, talking to a good-looking brunette who usually worked that side of the street. Rosa later told him that she'd had her eye on him and hoped he wouldn't go off with Carol, because he was the best type of man she'd seen in the time she had been on the game. If a girl could do it with men like him, she said, the job wouldn't be so bad. It was having to endure all shapes and sizes of men, and men of all ages, that got her down.

Rosa was well aware that she'd fallen a long way since she left Albury. A prostitute was as low as a woman could get, she believed. But that night, she saw Mr Wonderful cross the road and walk towards her. He's coming to me, she thought with a surge of interest. He was exactly the kind of man she'd always dreamt of meeting.

'You want something special, handsome?' she asked as Baxter walked up to her.

He looked down at her gaping cleavage and wondered for the umpteenth time why a nice-looking girl like this one would take up such a degrading business. 'Okay,' he said, thinking if he told her what he really wanted from her, she would probably refuse to leave the street. He'd have to wait until they got to her room.

It wasn't far to the flat Rosa shared with Prue and Alan. The rooms were better than Baxter expected, though the furnishings were garish.

'I'm Rosa, handsome,' she said, smiling seductively and batting her lashes. 'I won't be a minute.' She made a quick trip to the loo and then came back to the bedroom, reached down and started unzipping her skirt.

Baxter put up his hand to stop her. 'I didn't come here for sex. I want to talk to you and I'll pay you for your time. Is it a deal?'

'Are you a cop or a do-gooder?' Rosa asked, wide-eyed.

'I'm neither. I'm a writer. How much do you usually charge?'

'It depends. Sixty dollars for nothing special,' she said and shrugged.

Baxter fished out his wallet and extracted a hundred-dollar bill. He handed it to her and she took it, lifted the mattress and slid the note underneath.

She sat down on the edge of the bed and looked up at him. 'Are you from one of the papers? There's always someone from the papers or the telly poking their noses in up here. When they need a bit of news, they come to the Cross.'

'It's a famous place,' Baxter said and smiled. His smile

seemed to do a lot to put Rosa at ease, and she opened her bag and took out a cigarette.

'Do you have to smoke?' Baxter asked. 'I'd rather you didn't.'

'All right. You some kind of health freak?'

'In a way,' he said. 'I'm an athlete of sorts.'

'You're the healthiest-looking bloke I've seen in this place,' she said, running her eyes over him lasciviously. 'So what do you want to talk about?'

Later she'd tell Baxter that it was a new experience having a man who simply wanted to talk to her. Some men would talk a lot, but they always wanted sex.

'You're right, I am a journalist,' he explained, 'although I'd like to write books. I don't work for the gutter press but for a respectable broadsheet, and I'm working on an in-depth investigative piece. I've talked to some of the other girls and they've helped me a lot. I'd appreciate it very much if you'd help me too.'

Rosa stared into his eyes—it seemed she was still sizing him up. Then she shrugged again. 'You seem all right to me. You don't come across as a man who uses a girl badly and leaves her feeling rotten. How can I help you, mister?'

'I'm Greg. Greg Baxter.'

'What do I call you? Mr Baxter?'

'You can call me Greg. I'd like to know what influenced you to get started in this business. If I had to make a guess, I'd say you come from a good family and that you didn't plan on becoming a prostitute. So what went wrong?'

Rosa thought about this question for a while. 'No,' she said finally, in a quiet voice. 'I didn't plan on becoming a prostitute when I was going to school in Albury.'

She looked at Baxter, who was now sitting on the end of her bed. He was wearing new clothes, and he hoped he seemed clean, decent and honest, because that's what he was. And it seemed Rosa knew it, because the whole story fell out of her—Albury, her stepmother, Prue, Alan, heroin. And the endless men and their endless wants. 'Once you get on the roundabout,' she concluded with a sigh, 'it's hard to get off.'

Baxter nodded. 'Ever thought about trying to give it up?'

Rosa's hands clenched in her lap. 'What would I do?' she asked, her voice strained. 'Where would I go? I haven't got much money. I often don't have enough to buy food. That's when I have a slack week, and I need what I earn to buy heroin.'

'You must earn a fair amount?'

'Yeah, sometimes I do, especially when there's a Yank ship in port. But heroin costs big bikkies, mister.' She sounded tough, but her smile was sad. 'If I don't get it I'm a wreck and I can't work.'

'There's places you can go if you really want to get off the roundabout,' Baxter suggested. 'I can point you to them, if you'd like.'

Rosa shook her head and stared into the distance. He'd never seen a young woman look so lost and full of despair. 'I think I'm past all that,' she said. 'I've sort of given up. There's not many ways you can leave the game. One is by dying, and I've thought about that. That happens.'

Baxter nodded solemnly. 'But you're still here.'

She quirked a half-smile. 'I'm still here. Look, there's the odd girls who are married and do it to earn extra money. If I was lucky enough to be married to a decent fellow, I wouldn't do that to him. I've seen the odd girl get an offer of marriage.' She gave Baxter a hopeful look under her eyelashes. 'There's all kinds of men come here. There's men who've lost their wives or could never find a wife—and there's some who want to take it out on all women by being as rough as possible while they're with you.'

Baxter tensed, wishing he could get his hands on the bastards who'd hurt this lovely girl. 'I hope you can steer clear of them in future.'

'Tell me about it. And once you lose your looks and figure, you're ready for the scrapheap because most men won't look at an old piece. The younger, the better. A young girl fires them up. After a few years at this game, you get to look old.'

'What will you do then, Rosa?' Baxter asked gently.

She gave him a strange sort of smile as she got up off the bed. 'I reckon I won't live that long, Greg. The thing is, what do I have to live for now?'

'There might be more out there for you than you think,' Baxter said, getting to his feet too. 'Well, the hour's up.'

She looked him up and down again. 'You sure you don't want sex? You've paid me enough for it.'

'No thanks,' Baxter said, holding up both hands and taking a step away.

'All right.' Her smile was a little too bright. 'I'll have to go and earn some more money now.'

'Would you mind if I come again? I've got a few more questions.'

'Your money's as good as the next fella's.' Rosa's smile turned wicked. 'And if the other girls see you coming to me, my prestige will go through the roof.'

As they went down the stairs, a tall, tough-looking man passed them. He had long fair hair tied in a pigtail and a bony face with peculiarly hollow cheeks. Was *this* the man Rosa had described as being ruggedly handsome?

'Another client?' Baxter asked, to make sure.

'That's my, er, boyfriend. Alan.'

'The fellow who got you started on drugs?' Baxter asked harshly. 'The one who brings you heroin and takes your money?'

'Yeah, that's what he does, Greg. But he also looks after Prue and me—sees that the men do right by us. Anyway, see you around, handsome.'

CHAPTER SEVENTEEN

Baxter met with Rosa on two other occasions. Each time they went to the flat, where she did her best to answer his questions. On the second occasion, she told him she wasn't feeling very well, and he asked if she'd been eating decent food. She looked far too slender and, from what she told him, her meals were very hit-and-miss affairs.

Baxter asked if she'd like to have a meal with him. Not just any meal, but dinner at a top restaurant.

Rosa stared at him and frowned. 'You'd take me to a restaurant? In case you haven't noticed, I'm a prostitute.'

'You're also a human being,' he said. 'You look to me as if you could use a nice piece of underdone steak and some green vegetables.'

'Who's paying?' she asked, crossing her arms.

'Me,' he said and smiled.

'What's your angle, Greg? You should know by now that you don't have to take me out for a meal to have sex with me.'

'I know that, and *you* should know by now that I'm not looking for sex. I told you, I'm a writer. I'm interested in how you react in different situations.'

She gave him a steady look, then laughed softly. 'You're a queer bugger, Greg. Queer but nice. You're not a poofter?'

'Definitely not. So, have a meal with me?'

'It would have to be lunch. I'd miss too much custom at night, and Alan wouldn't like that. There's always some girl trying to take your spot, and they seem to be getting younger and younger.'

'All right, lunch. And there's just a couple of things I'll ask of you.'

She stiffened, her eyes turning suspicious. 'What?'

'Nothing much—just please don't wear a skimpy skirt like the one you've got on now, put on something that covers your top part, and don't overdo the makeup. Dress more like an office girl. Can you do that?'

'No worries,' she said, looking relieved. 'I'll do the best I can.'

'Thank you.' He scribbled out the address, added the phone number and handed it to her. 'You get a taxi and I'll pay for it. When can I expect you?'

'Tomorrow at noon?'

•

So that was how Frances Baxter came to meet Rosa.

Baxter hoped not only to get some nutritious food into her, but also that contact with another section of the community might cause her to think twice about carrying on her trade. When she arrived, he told her that she was being personally attended to by the woman who owned the restaurant. 'What a classy lady,' Rosa whispered, when she caught sight of Frances. Baxter didn't tell her that the classy lady was his mother.

The Great Woman smiled kindly as she presented Rosa with her most famous delicacies, setting the fine china down on the white tablecloth.

'It's lovely food but I can't eat all of it,' Rosa told Baxter under her breath, blushing with embarrassment while she picked at the meal. He could tell she was enjoying the taste, but years of deprivation had probably shrunk her stomach. At least the ice-cream dessert disappeared.

Dressed in her best clothes and wearing very little makeup, Rosa looked quite presentable. That was until one looked closely at her, which the worldly-wise Frances did. 'Rosa won't make old bones, Greg,' she said later, shaking her head.

Baxter sent Rosa back to the Cross in a taxi and said he'd see her in a few days.

•

The next time Baxter followed Rosa into her bedroom, he found Alan waiting. The pimp lunged at him with a knife.

Almost nonchalantly, Baxter pushed Alan's arm aside and slapped him hard on the face. Alan stumbled. But after managing to steady himself, he had another go, this time swinging his knife in a big arc. Baxter hit his arm midway between wrist and elbow—hit it so hard that the bone snapped. Alan's knife flew across the bed as he clutched his broken arm, folding at the knees and groaning in agony.

'Do you really like this creep?' Baxter asked with palpable contempt in his voice.

Rosa was standing as still as stone. 'How did you do that?' she gasped, watching Alan writhe and moan. 'Like he was a child. I've never seen him lose.' Then her amazement was quickly replaced by another emotion—it looked like fear. 'You'd better go, Greg,' she said shakily, starting to hustle him out of the bedroom. 'You can't be here anymore. I've got to take care of Alan. It looks like he needs a doctor.'

'He's fortunate he doesn't need an undertaker, Rosa.'

Baxter tried to stay where he was, but she was so insistent and he didn't want to hurt her or make her feel threatened. He let her push him from the room, then turned to her and asked, 'Why don't you dump the mongrel? He's nothing but a low-life parasite.'

But Rosa shook her head. Her face was pale and her whole body was trembling. 'You still don't understand how it is for me. Maybe you can't.'

'Rosa—'

'Just go, Greg,' she insisted. '*Please*.' With that, she went back into the bedroom, slammed the door and started soothing Alan. Baxter felt he had no choice but to leave.

•

A few days later, Greg and his mother were having dinner at the restaurant when the phone rang. It was a nursing sister at St Vincent's, asking for a Mr Greg Baxter.

'Yes, Sister, how can I help you?' Baxter asked.

'There's a girl here in a bad way—I believe her name is Rosa. Another girl, Prue, came with her and brought her handbag. There are a couple of phone numbers with your name next to them. I asked Prue about you, and she said Rosa trusts you and would want you to come in. Then Prue left—just up and left her friend.' The sister sighed. 'Well, I couldn't see the harm in contacting you.'

Baxter's heart was pounding. 'How bad is she?'

'Very bad,' the sister said gravely. 'She's overdosed on heroin.'

CHAPTER EIGHTEEN

'I'll come straight away,' Baxter said, slamming down the phone and rushing to pull on his jacket.

'What is it, Greg?' his mother asked. When he'd explained the situation, she touched him lightly on the arm and asked, 'Would you like me to come with you?'

'Would you do that?'

'Of course. You might need some support.' Frances picked up her handbag.

'You're a bottler, Mum,' Baxter said thickly.

'I'm your mother, Greg. This is a situation you can't solve with your martial arts.'

•

Rosa was a shocking colour and lay as still as death. Festooned with tubes, she no longer presented as a girl, but instead as some nightmarish form of life from another planet.

Baxter pulled up a chair beside the bed for his mother and then found another for himself. He sat down and cradled the girl's limp hand in his own.

'Rosa, this is my mother,' he said gently. 'Frances Baxter. It was her restaurant I took you to for lunch, and it was Mum who served us. When you get over this, there's a job waiting for you with her. You could learn to cook and maybe become a great chef. You just have to be brave and throw the habit, and I'll take you to where you can do that. You won't have to worry about that creepy Alan bothering you.'

Rosa's eyelids flickered and she opened her eyes briefly, saw Baxter and gave him what was clearly a smile. It was the smile of a young girl, and it was the last smile of her nineteen years of life.

Baxter and his mother sat with her until well into the early hours of the morning, when a Sister came in and shook her head.

Frances touched her son's shoulder. 'She's gone, Greg.'

'What a bloody awful way to die,' he said, his voice rough. 'Rosa should have had her family with her. She didn't even have her girlfriend because Prue was too busy screwing to get money to buy more heroin. God help this country if that's what it's come to. By God someone is going to pay for this.'

'Shh, Greg. You cared about her and I'm very proud of you.' Later Frances told him that she was prouder of her son at this moment than she had ever been.

•

Neither of them spoke on the drive home, as Frances handled the BMW in her usual efficient manner. 'I could use a drink, as late as it is,' she said when they arrived. 'And as much as you're against spirits, I think you could use a brandy, too, Greg.'

Baxter took the brandy his mother handed to him, his mind elsewhere. He thought that every kid who believed it was cool to use drugs should be forced to stand beside the bed of a drug victim as their life ebbed away.

Frances looked at him pensively. 'Why this girl, Greg? Why Rosa? Why was she different to the other street girls you talked to?'

'She reminded me of Elaine,' he admitted.

Frances sighed. 'Poor Elaine. You haven't had much luck with women, have you?'

'Not much. But you have to know, I never thought of Rosa as a girlfriend—only as a lost soul I'd have liked to save.' He drained his brandy. 'By God, I'm angry, Mum,' he said fiercely. 'There's a mountain of misery out there so some grubs can make a lot of money. They don't care, Mum. They just don't care.'

'Prostitution isn't a new development, Greg. It hasn't been called the oldest of professions for nothing. I happen to think that, as demeaning as it is for women, it serves a very useful purpose—and many women go on the game with their eyes open.'

'It's not the prostitution as such that disturbs me, so much as the way girls like Rosa and Prue are inveigled into it. Creeps like their pimp get them started on heroin and in no time at all, they're hooked. Then they've got no recourse but prostitution.'

Frances nodded. 'You're right, that's a terrible thing.'

'I didn't tell you, because I didn't want you to worry, but that grub who supplied Rosa with heroin, Alan, got it into his head that I was trying to take away one of his meal tickets. This was after Rosa had lunch with us. The creep came at me with a knife.'

'Oh, God,' Frances gasped, and gripped her son's arm. 'What happened?'

'I broke the mongrel's arm, that's what happened. It should have been his neck,' Baxter said savagely. 'For two pins I'd go back and give him a proper hiding.' Frances was alarmed, so he took a few deep breaths, calming himself. 'I'm going back there anyway. I need to tell Prue about Rosa. Maybe she knows where Rosa's people are.'

'I'll go with you, Greg,' Frances said quickly. 'In the mood you're in, I don't want you going there alone.'

'It's not a good scene, Mum.'

'I believe you, but I'm going anyway,' she said, her voice firm.

•

After a couple of hours' sleep and an early breakfast, Frances drove her son to Kings Cross. They parked in a street behind the girl's flat and walked the rest of the way.

The front entrance of the flats was open and they walked up the stairs to the first floor, where they found a tearful Prue lying on her bed. Alan, his arm in plaster, was sitting in a chair in an adjoining bedroom, smoking a cigarette. His face changed colour when he saw Baxter in the doorway—he looked like he'd seen a ghost. Then his eyes caught on Frances, who was very smartly dressed, her auburn hair in a neat bun.

'Is that a cop?' Alan asked and scowled, getting up and stubbing out his cigarette on a dirty ashtray. 'You brought a cop here?'

Baxter advanced into the room. 'Listen to me, you grub. One of your meal tickets died early this morning. My mother and I were the only ones with her.'

He heard Prue let out a loud wail and start sobbing, and then his mother's footsteps as she went to comfort the girl.

Alan didn't say anything, and he didn't look surprised. This seemed to confirm what Baxter had guessed—that Alan didn't belt Rosa to punish her, but kept her off heroin until she literally crawled to him for a fix. This time, when he'd given her the stuff, she'd gone away and promptly overdosed.

Baxter got right in the pimp's face. 'You've got one chance, and one chance only, to show you've got a trace of good in you. You've been living off these girls for more than two years. If you don't pay for Rosa to have a decent funeral, I'll come back here and there'll be another funeral . . . *YOURS*. Pray you never see me again, because if you do, you'll wish you'd never been born.'

Alan flinched and held up his hands, cowering. 'All right, all right.'

Baxter heard a noise and turned to see that Prue and Frances were standing in the doorway behind him, listening. Tears were rolling down Prue's face, her shoulders hitching. Baxter walked over to the women and closed the door on Alan. The three of them stood crowded together in the tiny living room.

'Prue, can you tell me if Rosa's father and stepmother are still alive and living in Albury?' he asked.

'I don't know,' she said between sobs. 'Probably.'

'Can you tell me Rosa's surname?'

'It's Craig. She was Rosa Craig.'

'Do you know what her father did?'

'He was some sort of a bigwig in the railway. Are you going to contact him?'

'We're going to try,' said Frances.

'Look, he wouldn't know anything about what Rosa's been doing,' Prue said urgently, gripping Baxter's arm. 'If you're thinking of getting him to come here for the funeral, you'd better not tell him what Rosa was doing or he might not come.'

'I won't tell him on the phone, but if I get him here, he'll have to know how his daughter came to be on the game. It can't be helped.'

'I suppose so,' Prue acknowledged, and let him go. 'Mister, I don't know why you're doing this, but I'm real pleased you are.'

'Get out of this game, Prue. The heroin will kill you just the same as it killed Rosa. Buck the habit and do something else.'

'I think it's too late for that,' she said.

'Baloney. You can do anything if you set your mind to it.' But then he realised his mum was shaking her head at him sadly, her eyes telling him to let it go. It seemed there was no use trying to reason with Prue. 'You'll be at the service?' he asked her.

'Of course. Rosa was my only real friend.'

•

Baxter rang Albury Police Station and told an officer that he needed to locate a man by the name of Craig, who held an executive position in the railway and whose daughter, Rosa, had left Albury about three years ago. Baxter provided his number and asked the officer to have Craig phone him directly.

Inside two hours Baxter's phone rang, with Ronald Craig at the other end. 'Mr Baxter? Albury police asked me to contact you with respect to my daughter, Rosa. Is there something I should know about her?'

'I'm afraid to say that your daughter passed away early this morning.'

There was a silence. Then Craig asked, in a rough voice, 'How?'

'I'd rather explain that in person.'

Impatience crept into Craig's tone. 'We've had very little news of her since she left here a few years ago. Who are you?' he demanded. 'What was she to you?'

'I wasn't Rosa's boyfriend, if that's what you're wondering. I'm a journalist and I met her while I was doing some research—'

'*Research?* On what?'

'It's a long story, Mr Craig. My mother and I were with Rosa when she died. She was taken to St Vincent's Hospital last night. Her friend Prue gave me your name.'

'You've seen Prue Hunter?'

'Yes, she and Rosa were flatmates. Prue's helping to organise Rosa's funeral. I don't have the details right now, but if you give me your phone number, I'll contact you. It's up to you, of course, whether you come or not.'

'I'll come,' Craig said curtly. 'Rosa was my daughter.'

A bit late to recognise that, Baxter thought.

●

No more than a dozen mourners attended Rosa's funeral, but at least there was a service. The church was beautifully decorated with flowers and greenery paid for by Frances Baxter. Half a dozen young women were present, and Baxter had talked with most of them at the Cross. There was, to his surprise, a female officer from the vice squad to whom he'd spoken on a couple of occasions.

At Baxter's insistence, Prue Hunter sat beside his mother and himself in the front pew. Ronald Craig sat with them.

Afterwards, Craig was invited to the Baxter house, where he was told of his daughter's fall from grace. Baxter gave Craig as much information as he knew, while Frances served coffee and cake, then looked on with sympathy in her eyes.

'I had no idea what Rosa was doing,' Craig said, tears in his eyes. 'She sent a card telling us that she was in Sydney, then one each Christmas. Nothing more.'

'I don't know the full story,' said Baxter, 'only what Rosa told me, but I'm sure she and Prue didn't leave Albury to become prostitutes.'

'Yes, you're right,' Craig said, his head in his hands. 'She just wanted a better life for herself, more independence. Everything was all right until I remarried. Jo and Rosa didn't get on, and I probably sided too much with Jo. She was too hard on Rosa. My poor daughter. She wouldn't take it anymore and cleared out.'

'If it's any comfort,' Frances said soothingly, 'you aren't by any means the only father this has ever happened to.'

'That's true,' Baxter put in. 'There have been a great many girls who finished up like Rosa, and there's heaps more unaccounted for.'

'Thank you, both of you, but the fact is that my Rosa is gone, and I shouldn't have turned my back on her. I've learned my lesson too late. You should never turn your back on your kids, especially when they need you.'

•

Baxter was sick to the stomach of the whole sorry mess. He felt great admiration for social workers and charity organisations—if it weren't for their efforts, the situation would be far worse. As it was, hundreds of people died from drug abuse each year.

A lot of it, Baxter believed, could be sheeted home to uncaring and irresponsible parents. There was Ronald Craig—a man in an executive position—who'd allowed his younger second wife to assume responsibility for his teenage daughter, and who hadn't been concerned enough about her when she'd left to try and locate her. Craig had been unbelievably slack, and now his daughter was dead. It was such a waste of a life.

Baxter had seen enough of Sydney's seamy side to last him all his life. His final conversation with Mr Garland had been swimming around in his head for days.

Although I won't be here to see it, the old man had said, *I reckon that one day you'll return to Moondilla. That's the kind of young man I think you are. You'll come back here and do things that people remember.*

'This is the finish of Sydney for me, Mum,' Baxter told her that night.

'What do you mean, Greg?'

'As soon as I can, I'm going to move back to Moondilla. Sydney might be all things for some people, and I know you love it here, but I want some peace and quiet. And the truth is, I've dreamt of returning to the town ever since we left.'

'You should think about this a bit longer, Greg,' Frances advised. 'Right now you're in an emotional trough.'

He shook his head and tried to sound firm enough to convince her. 'No, that isn't it. I don't want to leave you, Mum, but I'm going to have to. I need to distance myself from Sydney. I want to go back to where fishing rates higher than heroin.'

Of course, he'd known that Moondilla wasn't Brigadoon—the unchanging town of Scottish myth—but he couldn't have known just how much it had changed.

CHAPTER NINETEEN

It was a jewel of a Sunday morning. There was a heavy dew and every drop of moisture seemed shot through with irradiated light. The early fog over the river had evaporated in the sunlight, and now a very blue sky contrasted against the lush green banks of the river.

Baxter had packed his Esky with tucker and taken it down to the *Flora Jane* before Steve Lewis arrived. He also loaded a big plastic container of water, mostly for Chief, and the dog's stainless-steel water bowl. They'd filled up the tank two nights before, when Lewis and his family had dropped by Riverview for dinner, and the engine started immediately.

'Sweet as apple pie,' Lewis said and smiled as he listened to the engine's beat.

'You do the steering, Steve,' Baxter suggested. 'You know

where you're going and the best way to get there, and I'm still on a learning curve.'

Lewis nodded and climbed into the boat. 'You'll definitely need a bit of practice to learn how to handle her in the swell.'

There was no one else out on the river at this early hour. Out beyond the river's mouth, several boats were kellicked close to the shore of the southern promontory that formed one arm of Moondilla's harbour. Steve waved to the occupants of some of these boats and then headed the boat out into the bay.

'What would they be fishing for?' Baxter asked.

'Blackfish, maybe. They're using light rods, so it would be that or bream. Some of those blokes might've been out all night. You need green weed to catch blackfish, as they have a tiny mouth. You use very small hooks, too. The others would be fishing for anything they could get . . . flathead, maybe the odd snapper.'

The boat didn't begin to rock until they left the harbour and came under the influence of the ocean's ceaseless swell. Lewis steered for the Islands and Baxter saw them up close for the first time: a group of large rocky outcrops, six in number, separated by channels of varying width. This was the favourite place of the more intrepid fishermen, because fish congregated around the bases of the outcrops. Weeds, kelp and cunjevoi grew thickly there and attracted a wide variety of sea life.

If a nor'easter was blowing, the shot was to get in behind one of the islets so as to stay in the relatively calmer water, because each islet acted as a block to the wind and current.

If there was a run-in tide, the drill was to try and kellick to a rock and fish on the Moondilla side—that is, with the boat's prow pointed towards Moondilla harbour. But how and where you fished, Lewis had explained, really depended on the wind and the tide and being aware of both.

There was no telling what kind of fish you might catch. You might come away with a young shark or—depending on your bait and the strength of your line—even an older and larger shark. Not that amateur fishermen wanted sharks, which most regarded as a damned nuisance, but the trawlers caught plenty and sold them too. They were marketed under different names, so most people who bought shark flesh didn't realise what they were eating. It was pretty good tucker with chips anyway.

Around the Islands you had to be very careful that you didn't allow your boat to be thrown up against a rock. This was most likely to happen if you fished on the open or ocean side, because a freak wave could come out of nowhere. Most fishermen didn't head to the ocean side unless there was a westerly wind blowing strongly from shore, which tended to flatten out the sea—at least to some extent. Every small child who fished with his or her father learned the facts of ocean fishing very quickly.

'We'll put in an hour or so here while the wind is down,' Lewis said, 'and if it stays down we'll head over to the northern point and have a lash there. I've got some fish berley and I could drop some here, but it's not a lot of help in deep water as the current washes it away so quickly.'

He was working away as he spoke, his voice loud and brimming with enthusiasm.

'I've also got some prawns and whole bait fish, as well as the lures. It's not a good place for lures—you lose too many and they're not cheap. I'll throw in a couple of light lines and see if I can hook some tiddlers for bait. First, I'll bait up a line and get you started.'

Baxter nodded and kept watching Lewis at work, taking it all in.

Then his mate paused and glanced at him. 'How are you handling the swell?'

'No problem. I don't feel sick at all,' Baxter said and grinned. He found he loved being out here—he loved the salty breeze, the blue sky and the view of the land. It seemed as far from the grit of Sydney as he could get.

'That's a relief,' said Lewis. 'Some people can't take this swell. It never stops when you're on the ocean. It's just that some days it's bigger than usual. The tide is about two hours off the turn. It's on the run-out, so it will take your line out pretty fast.' Lewis shot Baxter another glance. 'How do you reckon Chief's handling things?'

'He's all right. The swell doesn't seem to be worrying him,' Baxter said, as he looked at his dog lying in the cabin. 'He'd complain if he didn't feel well.'

Lewis threw out some berley of chopped-up fish, prawns, pollard and bread, and dropped two light lines down alongside *Flora*. Then he hooked a bait fish through the tail and cast out on the opposite side of the boat to Baxter's line. It had hardly hit the water, or so it seemed, than Lewis announced that he had a strike.

'Shall I have a go reeling in, Steve?' Baxter asked.

'Might be as well. Appears to be a fair fish.'

Baxter began to reel, then saw his own line tighten and announced that he too had a fish hooked.

'How big?' Lewis asked.

'I can handle him okay.'

'That doesn't tell me anything! We're not all powerhouses. But if you can bring him in alone, do it. I've got a big one and it may take a while to land him.'

It took longer than Baxter expected to reel in his snapper, because it was certainly a decent-sized fish. Lewis was still fighting his catch.

'What type do you reckon it is, Steve?' Baxter asked.

'It feels like a bloody great shark. Ever used a gaff?'

'Never. What do I do?'

'Hook it when I get the bugger alongside and then hold on real tight,' Lewis explained. 'Don't lean over too far or you could end up in the water.'

'I see it,' Baxter said as his mate's fish rose to the surface for a second.

'So do I. I think it's a jewie. They call them mulloway now. They eat pretty well.'

Baxter pulled it in with the gaff, and Lewis said he reckoned it would go close to twenty kilos.

•

Inside two hours the men had caught fifteen good-sized fish, including two ugly red rock cod. When Baxter brought up the first one he said he'd toss it back, but Lewis stopped him. 'No fear, Greg. They're great eating fish. They only look ugly.'

Baxter was enjoying himself no end—and when he hooked what he thought might be the biggest fish of the morning, he felt really good.

It took some battling to get it to the boat, and he was hugely disappointed when Lewis shook his head and announced that he was going to cut the line.

'Why?' Baxter asked urgently.

'It's a tiger shark—we don't want it.'

'Ah, all right.' Baxter noticed something. 'I think that might be his momma or poppa out there,' he said, pointing to where a triangular-shaped fin was cleaving the water on the port side of the boat. The last fish Lewis had caught had been bitten in half, which they'd attributed to a shark—it seemed they'd been right.

Then Baxter realised that Lewis couldn't see the fin because he had his back turned and was too caught up with dislodging the emasculated fish on his line. 'Let's pull off, Greg. The wind's starting to strengthen and we've got enough fish for one outing.'

Chief, who'd come out from under the cabin, had his nose pointed into the wind. He barked twice—the kind of bark he employed to warn of approaching vehicles.

Obviously there were no cars, but Baxter had become so used to every nuance of the dog's behaviour that he immediately looked at the shepherd to find out why he was concerned. 'What is it, mate?'

Chief barked again with his nose towards the next islet.

What Baxter saw now made him shiver. 'Steve, there's a body hooked on the rocks over there. That's what the sharks are after.'

CHAPTER TWENTY

Lewis turned quickly and looked at where Baxter's finger was pointing. 'Jesus wept, you're right.' He put down his rod and started the engine. It kicked into life and he steered *Flora* about in a gentle turn. 'I don't like the look of this, Greg.'

'Neither do I,' Baxter said grimly. He was thinking of the undercover policewoman's body and its discovery by fishermen. What if this body turned out to be Latham's? From this distance, its clothes and its shape looked male.

Then he remembered what Lewis had said about Julie the other day. *Those baggy jeans or shorts and a man's shirt she gets around in—from a distance you'd swear blind she was a bloke.* Baxter's heart clenched. Surely it wasn't her.

'We can't just leave it out here,' he said, and Lewis nodded.

'I'll use my radio and have the police at the wharf by the time we're back with the body in tow.'

'Lucky you brought it, Steve.'

'No luck about it. I never go out here without it—you never know when you might need to send a distress call.'

Once Lewis had contacted shore, he took the boat out of the protection afforded by their islet, and into the channel between it and its neighbour. They could immediately feel the difference in the level of swell. Baxter watched on in admiration as Lewis manoeuvred *Flora* towards the other islet. The body came into clearer view.

'It's a man,' Baxter shouted to Lewis at the wheel of the boat. 'That's all I can tell.'

He was ashamed to feel a thrill of relief, but he couldn't help it. Julie was safe.

'You'll have to try and hook the gaff into his clobber, Greg. Do it as quickly as you can. The swell will push us hard onto the rocks if we stuff around.'

Baxter hadn't the slightest intention of stuffing around—he wanted to vacate the Islands as quickly as possible.

The body was lodged facedown on a snag of rock that ran out into the sea from the islet proper. This ridge had been exposed by the run-out tide—it was sure to be covered at full tide. As the boat nosed alongside, Baxter leaned out, got the gaff hooked in the body's belt and pulled it from the ridge. He could see now that one arm had been bitten off below the shoulder.

'I've got him,' Baxter said, 'so go for your life. Let's hope the shark doesn't have another crack at him—it's taken off one arm already.'

'Good man, Greg.'

Lewis pointed the boat down the channel between the islets and then, using them as some protection against the swell, he steered directly for Moondilla's wharf, where the fishing fleet usually moored. The shark followed them for some distance, but didn't come any closer. After a few minutes it disappeared.

'The shark appears to have left us,' Baxter said.

'As long as it doesn't come up underneath us. If you feel something get at the body, you'll have to try and lift it into the boat. Think you can do that?'

'No worries.'

'Don't try it unless you have to—the weight of you plus the body could tip you in. Good thing we'll be at the wharf in a few minutes.'

Baxter hoped the bloody shark would keep away. A few bites could make a real mess of the body, and make identification more difficult for the police.

The shark didn't reappear, but Baxter's strength and resilience were beginning to feel the strain of holding the bloated body against the boat. Wanting to distract himself, he looked to shore and saw two police cars tearing down the beach road, their lights flashing, before they pulled up at the wharf.

Lewis had noticed them too. 'The boys in blue are waiting for us, Greg.'

'It's some place, this Moondilla. Never a dull moment,' Baxter said dryly.

'You've got to admit we had a good morning's fishing. And not many fishermen return with a human body on their gaff,' Lewis said, his smile grim.

Baxter gave him a weak grin. 'Do you know of anyone who's been reported missing?'

'No locals. It could be a bloke off a freighter—plenty of them go up and down this coast. Maybe he drank too much and fell overboard.'

Lewis took *Flora* in alongside the jetty and as close to the beach as he could without grounding her. There were quite a few civilians on the beach, but the police had cleared the wharf and a uniformed officer stood at the entrance to prevent anyone accessing it.

Three other officers were waiting on the wharf just above the boat. Baxter threw his forward mooring rope up to one of them, who managed to catch it and make it fast to a pylon. Lewis cut the motor and then left the cabin to help Baxter lift the body from the sea. A grim task, though the stink wasn't too bad because of the salt water. Chief watched with great interest, but didn't go near the body.

Once they had it in the boat, they took an end each and lifted it up to the waiting trio of officers, who turned it onto its back.

Lewis swore very loudly. 'Bloody hell.' Despite everything the body had been put through, its face was still intact enough to recognise up close. 'It's Jack Drew,' Lewis said, and Baxter agreed.

The two men looked at each other in amazement.

CHAPTER TWENTY-ONE

'Was Drew missing?' Baxter asked the police trio.

'Mrs Drew phoned us yesterday morning and said that Jack hadn't come home,' a young two-striper answered. He was addressing himself to Lewis, whom he seemed to know and be on good terms with. 'Considering Jack's history, we weren't too worried.'

'You didn't worry he was lost at sea?' Lewis asked, his eyebrows raised.

'No, because he wasn't fishing. Well, he had been, earlier in the day, but he was at the Family Hotel in the evening. Before he left for the pub, he told his wife that he needed to meet someone there. That was the last she saw of him.'

Another police car pulled up at the wharf, followed by an

ambulance. Two more officers walked along the jetty to join the trio around the body.

One was Senior Sergeant Cross, and Baxter was disturbed to realise that he seemed to be the highest-ranking officer of the group.

•

Baxter and Lewis gave verbal accounts of their discovery of Drew's body and its exact location. The investigation heated up when Julie, in her capacity as medical examiner, carried out the post-mortem. Her findings brought more coppers to Moondilla—some came from Bega, while two plainclothes detectives drove down from Sydney.

Julie's post-mortem revealed that the back of Drew's skull had been crushed in several places. By drawing a long bow, it was possible to conclude that this damage had been caused by his head coming into contact with rocks at the Islands—but Julie didn't think this was a feasible explanation. It might have been tenable if there'd been only one or two major depressions in Drew's skull, but there were at least a dozen. It seemed someone had made certain that Jack Drew was dead before dumping his corpse out at sea.

Both Baxter and Lewis were asked to present themselves for further questioning at the police station. The coppers didn't waste much time talking to Lewis. He answered a few questions, signed a statement and left.

Baxter was treated very differently. He was led into an

interview room, the kind used for suspects being interrogated about a crime. It was featureless except for a one-way window, and the drab grey walls weren't conducive to raising one's spirits.

There were three police officers in the room. Two sat facing Baxter, and a third—Senior Sergeant Cross—sat against one wall. It seemed Cross seldom smiled; he reminded Baxter of a crow waiting to pick up scraps. He certainly did nothing to lighten the mood. The two plainclothes detectives wore suits and ties, and presented a much better image. They introduced themselves and told Baxter they'd come from Sydney.

One asked questions while the other took notes. The substance of the interrogation went as follows:

'Mr Baxter, can you account for your movements last Friday evening?'

'If I have to, but I don't see the relevance. Your question is ill-directed.'

'Let us be the best judges of the question's relevance. We have information that you were seen in the vicinity of the Family Hotel at about the time Jack Drew left it. That was between six-thirty and seven p.m.'

Baxter laughed loudly. 'Is that the best you can come up with? Your informant needs his eyes checked, and you should check your facts more carefully. Are you implying it was me who killed Jack Drew?'

'How well do you know Elizabeth Drew?'

'I can't say that I know her very well, as I've met her only twice,' Baxter said. 'The first time, she and Drew were having an argument in the Family Hotel—he backhanded her and knocked her down. I picked her up and then I told Drew he was a mongrel to hit a woman. He threw a punch at me and I decked him. Then I drove Mrs Drew home.'

'Subsequently you had another fight with Drew, didn't you?'

'I wouldn't describe it as a fight. Drew came out to my place, mouthing off about what he was going to do to me. He was sober this time and he told me he was going to give me a hiding.'

'So you broke his ribs and put him in hospital?'

'That's right. He attacked me and I defended myself. I gave him first aid, called an ambulance and then rang his wife. The second time I met Liz, she came out to pick up her car, accompanied by Julie—by Dr Rankin.'

The detectives glanced at each other. 'And you haven't seen Liz Drew since then, or spoken to her on the phone?'

'I've spoken to her, yes—she called to thank me for fixing her husband. If you're implying that I had a reason to kill Drew because of a liaison with his wife, you're way off the mark. I had nothing against the man personally. He was simply an ex-pug who thought he was king of the heap and could get away with just about anything. I don't have any regard for men who knock women about, and Drew paid the price for that.'

'You haven't said why you were in town Friday evening.'

'That's because I wasn't in town. At the specific time you refer to, I was having dinner with the Lewis family at my house out by the river. Even Jesus Christ couldn't be in two places at the same time,' Baxter added, with biting sarcasm.

The note-taking detective got up and left the room. He returned in a few minutes and whispered in the ear of the detective conducting the interrogation.

'It seems your story checks out,' the interviewer said.

Baxter noticed a scowl appear on Cross's face, before his expression became carefully blank. Cross was a decent actor, but not quite good enough.

'Of course it checks out,' Baxter said. 'You fellows are way off the mark and wasting your time talking to me. It was a pretty hairy job getting Drew's body off the rocks and with that bloody great shark close by. I had to gaff him in a good-sized swell and then hold him next to the boat the whole way in.'

At that description, the detectives both looked a bit green about the gills.

'If you're finished,' Baxter said, 'I'll go now.'

'We're nearly done,' the interviewer said. 'Just a few more minutes.'

Baxter looked at each of the three officers, his eyes lingering on Cross. 'I haven't been here long,' he said, 'but it's common knowledge that a certain well-known person in this town was out to get Jack Drew. This person has the hots for Mrs Drew. I'll bet that he and the fellow who gave you the false and misleading information about my movements are one and the same. Or that the informant is a close associate of his. Either way, he's the one you should be grilling.'

'Why would this man pick on you?'

'Because I make a good fall guy to take suspicion off the bloke or blokes who killed Drew,' Baxter said. 'Then there's the fact that I publicly humiliated him.'

'How did you do that?'

Baxter allowed himself a small smirk. 'He tried to deck me, so I gave him a kick in the behind. Ask anyone in town—it's common knowledge.'

The note-taking detective handed him a sheet of paper on which were drawn the six islets of the Islands. Then the interviewer said, 'Mr Lewis told us that this cross marks the spot where you sighted Drew's body and from which you recovered it. Is that your reading of the correct location?'

'Absolutely,' Baxter agreed, smiling. 'There's only one small discrepancy.'

'Yes, what's that?'

'Neither Steve nor I actually discovered Drew's body. It was my dog Chief who noticed him—Chief's got a fantastic sense of smell. Us blokes were too busy reeling in and cutting my line because there was a tiger shark on it. Chief barked and pointed his nose towards the next islet, and I looked and saw the body. That's if you're interested in getting the story absolutely correct. If my dog hadn't barked, we might have left Drew where he was. It's a tricky place to be with a decent swell running.'

'Thank you,' the interviewer said, keeping his tone professional although his lips were tugging up at the corners. 'You did a great job getting Drew's body back here. I doubt we'll need to talk to you again.'

'I hope not, because you'd be wasting more of your time.' This seemed to Baxter like a good opportunity to find out more. 'Nobody's told me,' he said, 'but I'm interested to know how Drew died. What killed him?'

'The back of his head was crushed. He'd been hit many times with something heavy, like a piece of pipe or a club of some description.'

Baxter immediately thought of Verna Graham's husband, Bob. *He was found with a fractured skull. It supposedly happened when he fell overboard.*

'He was, eh?' Baxter asked. 'Hit from behind? Maybe by someone who wouldn't face him front-on. I sure hope you nail the creep. Drew wasn't a great man by any stretch, but he didn't deserve to end up the way he did. And the talk was that he'd improved since the last walloping I gave him. Liz certainly thought so.'

Just before Baxter left the room, one of the plainclothes detectives winked at him. This made him wonder if the entire interrogation had been a 'snow' job—after all, the whole thing had been utterly absurd.

While Campanelli had probably tried to fit him for Jack Drew's murder, it had been a very amateurish attempt. What concerned Baxter was what might happen next.

Once outside the police station he made a beeline for Moondilla Motors.

'How did you finish up with the fuzz?' Lewis asked, wiping engine grease from his hands. 'I heard from Jane that they called her to confirm your alibi.'

Baxter told him the whole story, including his suspicions. Then their talk wandered back to fishing and plans to revisit the Islands. When Baxter thanked Lewis for taking him out on the boat and showing him the ropes, and asked if he could return the favour, Lewis mentioned that Jason might want some martial arts lessons. That sounded fine to Baxter—he reckoned he could help the boy get into shape.

'Well, I'd best head off,' Baxter said, looking at his watch. 'Julie's going to run me home. I left Chief with her and he'll be worried about me.'

CHAPTER TWENTY-TWO

Chief stood on the back seat of Julie Rankin's car with his head between the front seats, enjoying himself as his master gave him scratches behind the ears. Baxter was incredibly proud of the shepherd for spotting Drew's body.

Baxter didn't say much on the short drive out to Riverview, and he noticed Julie glancing at him several times. 'You okay, Greg?' she asked at last.

'I'm okay, Julie. Just lost in thought about Jack Drew and Moondilla. It's all a damned shame. Mum will soon be telling me "I told you so". She said I wouldn't find it the same sleepy, peaceful place it was when we lived here.'

'Well, you'll be pleased to hear I've got some good news.' Julie smiled. 'I contacted Ian Latham today, and he told me that they're on the verge of catching the drug peddlers. So I wouldn't worry too much about that, Greg.'

'That's terrific news,' Baxter said, returning her smile for a moment. Then he sobered again. 'They might clean them up here, but there'll always be drug pushers. The big money gets them in.'

Julie sighed. 'True enough.'

They were approaching Riverview. 'You can drop me at the gate and I'll jog from there,' Baxter said, expecting her to want to head back to work.

But when Julie braked and pulled up, she turned to him and said, 'Jack Drew wasn't involved in drugs. Not that we know of, anyway.'

'Drew's murder was probably for a very different reason. Someone told me that it's common knowledge Campanelli had sworn to "get" Drew.'

'That's the story, Greg. But why would Campanelli risk his position here for someone like Jack Drew? It doesn't make sense.'

'It doesn't have to make sense. Sometimes it's revenge and sometimes it's an ego thing: "I'm top of the heap and nobody makes me look small and gets away with it." That's the code of the Mafia. Maybe Campanelli needed to exert himself to pull others into line. He's playing for big stakes. Add the fact that he has the hots for Liz—well, he could kill two birds with one stone.'

'Three birds, if he'd been able to frame you for murder as part of the bargain.'

Julie's eyes flashed with anger, it seemed on Baxter's behalf. He wanted to reach out and take her hand, but instead decided a change of topic was needed.

'How is Liz taking Jack's death?' he asked.

'Not very well. You'd imagine that she might be relieved to be rid of him, after the way he knocked her around, but they liked each other well enough when he was sober—and as far as I know, he hadn't been on the grog since that last beating you gave him.'

Baxter nodded. 'Yes, Liz told me that.'

'The other thing is, she's frightened of Campanelli,' Julie said gravely. 'She knows he wants her, and that he has a bad reputation with women. I think she even saw him in action on one occasion. She's dead scared he'll come for her now she hasn't got her husband to protect her. I've had to give her some sedatives to calm her down.'

Baxter fought to control his anger. 'I'd like to get my hands on the mongrel.'

'Well, you're not the only one. Even though she's terrified, Liz told me she wanted to front Campanelli and have it out with him.'

'*What?*'

'It makes a kind of sense. She said that since he was going to come for her anyway, why shouldn't she go to him first? She's absolutely convinced that Jack was killed by him or one of his men. I advised her not to do anything so silly—to stay right away from the big devil and leave it to the police to handle. From what Latham said, he'll probably get Campanelli before anything can happen to Liz.'

'She's a great style of woman,' Baxter said, 'but how did she come to marry Jack Drew? You said you might tell me sometime.'

'The novelist's curiosity?' Julie asked with raised eyebrows.

'To some extent. Not that I can describe myself as a novelist just yet, but I'm learning more and more that people—with their hopes and fears and foibles—are the foundation stones a writer must build on to create a story. The more thoroughly you dissect those core elements, the better you write. So I'm wondering: what motivated a woman with Liz's looks and background to marry an ex-pug and a boozer to boot?'

'I *could* tell you, Greg . . . but I'd prefer that you got it directly from Liz.'

'Spoilsport. But you're probably right. Besides, what red-blooded male would turn down the opportunity for a couple of hours' chinwag with the smashing Liz Drew?'

He was hoping Julie might reveal some jealousy at that, but she just laughed and said, 'Liz thinks you're the ant's pants, so I'm sure she won't buck at a chinwag with you.'

Concealing his disappointment, Baxter said he should probably head up to the house and let Julie go on her way. 'Many thanks for the lift,' he added.

'Any time. Remember your fish!'

He got out and opened the door for Chief, then pulled out the Esky full of fish that Lewis had given him back at the garage.

Just before Baxter closed the car door, he remembered he had something important to ask Julie. 'Mum's arriving tomorrow—'

'Monday?' Julie interrupted, her brow furrowed in momentary confusion, then, 'Oh, of course, she's in the restaurant business!'

'Yes, she's staying Monday till Friday. I know she'd love to meet you, so how about dinner Tuesday? That's your night off, isn't it? We'll cook you a meal of red rock cod. Ugliest fish I've ever seen, but Steve assures me they're very good eating.'

CHAPTER TWENTY-THREE

Greg Baxter did not stand in awe of many people, but he was in awe of his mother.

Frances Baxter was an icon of the culinary world. She created an indelible impression wherever she went and whenever she spoke. Over the past few decades she'd become a byword in the hospitality business, owning a series of internationally famous restaurants. Her current establishment in Sydney was a destination for fine-diners from Japan to Paris to New York. Her cookery books were all bestsellers, and at least two were mandatory for any aspiring hosts of a truly memorable dinner party.

Over the years, Frances had visited nearly every country that could boast of an authentic cuisine. It didn't matter if the meat was lamb, pork, beef, fish, chicken, kangaroo or alpaca, she knew more ways to present it than just about anyone anywhere.

Baxter was very proud of his mother's achievements. He'd never sought the kind of publicity that had characterised her life, but he understood why it was meat and drink to her. It brought people to her restaurants, created a demand for her books and helped to make her fabulously wealthy.

And beneath the gloss of her persona, Frances was a decent woman. She treated her employees well and donated money to several charities. Her decency was what had always awed and inspired her son most of all.

•

Frances had been born with two essential traits for success: the first was a love of cooking and the second was entrepreneurial ability of a high order.

As a small child she spent hours with her mother in the kitchen. She started with simple things like cupcakes and pikelets, and gradually moved on to more difficult recipes. By the age of ten she could make sponges and fruit cakes that won at the local shows, and the name Frances Reid soon became known around the district. Whenever she had a spare moment, the teenage Frances had her head in a cookery book.

When the local café came on the market, Frances' parents bought it and with it the opportunity for their daughter to widen her scope. She helped her father and mother prepare meals, and was soon doing much of the cooking. The café was also materially helped by the fact that Frances was very attractive in looks and personality.

When her parents were killed in a car accident, Frances carried on running the café. It grew extremely popular with trawlermen, as she purchased the best fish and seafood. A meal at the café became a ritual for many people, both local and visiting.

One man, in particular, never failed to have one or two meals a week at Frances' café. He was a moderately wealthy man who played the stock exchange and lived in Moondilla because he spent most of his spare time fishing.

Richard Baxter had lost his first wife and was ten years older than Frances, but she married him. She could tell he thought she was something special—he didn't try to change her. And he purchased the building adjoining the café, which allowed her to cater for more diners and for wedding functions.

Having a baby hardly caused Frances to miss a beat, and she carried on supervising the café almost to the day of Greg's birth. She'd hoped for a girl but she wasn't at all disappointed with her ten-pound baby son—Richard was the one who felt overwhelmed by parenthood.

Greg was six when Frances and Richard made the decision to sell the café and move to Sydney. Business at their new restaurant was helped by some well-chosen TV segments, and before long they were receiving more bookings than they could handle.

When Richard died suddenly of a heart attack, Frances' way of handling her grief was to sell her restaurant and purchase another. It was here that she came up with an inexpensive but nutritious lunch for nine-to-fivers, which attracted a lot of attention on television. In one of many interviews at this time, she was first referred to as the Great Woman: 'Yes, viewers, the Great Woman herself is here with us today.'

Chuffed at the popularity of her lunches, Frances tried something new. She incorporated a semi-luxury dining unit into her restaurant that could be utilised by government and business VIPs for special meetings. There was a special back entrance for private admittance, and the unit could be rented for an hour or a day. If you were especially famous, you might be attended by Frances herself, but otherwise by discreet employees whom she'd personally trained. After a meal, the VIPs could relax in super-comfortable lounge chairs while carrying on their business.

Suffice to say that a great many important 'deals' were discussed and agreed to in this unit. It was expensive, but it was what the top people wanted and were used to—and a legitimate tax deduction. Clearly, Frances was a great lateral thinker.

She became a guest on countless TV and radio talk shows, and was soon one of Australia's most recognisable women. It wasn't difficult to understand her popularity in this arena. Some called it a sparkling personality, some called it charisma— whatever it was, the handsome woman with warm brown eyes and gleaming auburn hair had it. When the Great Woman spoke about a dish, people everywhere wanted a taste.

•

Despite her success and the busy nature of her life, Frances spent as much time as possible with young Greg. She'd very much wanted a daughter, but there were no more babies—this wasn't her fault, but her husband's—so all her motherly love had been channelled into her son. Baxter never for one moment in his life had felt neglected, and he'd never entertained any doubt that his mother loved him.

Just like his mother, he learned to cook early, although it never became an obsession with him. Instead his interest in gymnastics blossomed, followed by a devotion to martial arts. Despite not understanding this—or why her son felt he had to travel to Japan and Korea to hone his skill in the latter field—Frances fully supported him. Subsequently she watched him demolish three crims who tried to rob her restaurant—it was a big night and there was quite a lot of money in the till. After that performance, Frances felt that her support of her son was well worthwhile.

And when Baxter told her he was leaving Sydney to live in Moondilla, Frances may not have thought it a wise move, but she still helped him buy the riverfront property he'd set his heart on acquiring. Not only was it a good investment, she told him, but she could see that he had to either get the writing bug out of his system or succeed at it before he would contemplate marriage.

Baxter had several friends who'd made disastrous marriages and he had no intention of following suit: he reckoned the old adage 'Marry in haste and repent in leisure' was absolutely true. Ideally, he favoured another two or three years on his own before thinking about wedded bliss. That would give him the time to get his first book published and a second one well on the way.

He knew his mother wasn't on board with these plans. She would always love to cook, but in recent years a new obsession had developed: grandchildren. Everything depended on her only child, so she did everything she could to hasten his progress. Baxter couldn't have been more aware of this, as he'd told Julie.

What he hadn't told Julie was that his mother had 'unearthed' several potential daughters-in-law, all of whom he'd rejected as 'unsuitable'. This had been particularly disappointing to Frances, because the young women in question dined at her restaurant on a regular basis and were regarded as belonging to 'the cream of the crop'.

Despite the fact that Greg had a mind of his own, Frances never failed to let her son know that she was very proud of him. He'd presented her with most of his trophies and plaques when he moved to Moondilla, and she'd told him on the phone that these were now displayed prominently in her Killara home and shown off to guests.

While she freely acknowledged that Greg developed peculiar ideas at times—like going off to Moondilla to write—Frances often told him that if this was the worst thing he ever did, she felt she'd never have reason to complain. She was glad he didn't smoke, drink or take drugs, and she not-so-secretly believed that she'd raised the most handsome and charming man in the world.

•

Frances had been aware that her son liked Julie Rankin ever since he'd been down in the dumps when she left his class for postgraduate study in London. In turn, Baxter was aware that his mother was aware of this. Whenever he turned down one of the young ladies she'd 'unearthed', she would bring up Elaine and Julie as the only women he'd ever really liked—and remind him that because both were out of his reach, he might just need to settle for someone else.

Now that Julie had surfaced in Moondilla, Frances' tune had changed—particularly when she'd learned that Greg was seeing the doctor quite frequently. They even *fished* together, she'd heard from an old friend in town.

In one of her many phone calls, the Great Woman told her son that she was quite disappointed he himself hadn't informed her of this state of affairs. She then asked if he was serious about Julie. Baxter hadn't known what to say.

'Well, are you or are you not serious about that woman?'

'It's not me, Mum. It seems Julie has a thing about men,' he tried to explain.

'A thing? What do you mean "a thing"?'

'It seems she prefers fishing to cuddling.'

'Good heavens. And have you cuddled her at all?'

'No, I don't want to spoil what we have. It's not a relationship—we're just good friends—but it's all right. I enjoy her company and she appears to enjoy mine.'

Of course Baxter knew—and Frances made it plain—that this was a setback to his mother's hopes. And it was soon after this conversation that she proposed her visit, an unmistakably optimistic tilt to her voice. Baxter was keen to see his mother, so the knowledge that she had an ulterior motive didn't bother him too much. He also believed that one meal with Julie would be enough to show Frances, once and for all, that there was no hope of grandchildren from that corner.

CHAPTER TWENTY-FOUR

Frances hugged and kissed her son, then asked him to help bring in her things from the car. It turned out she'd packed the boot and back seat with a fine range of culinary goodies and condiments, as well as a case of expertly selected wine and liquor—all items which she believed that Baxter wouldn't be able to afford on his tight budget.

'It seems you're living largely on fish,' she said, 'which is fine and which I, personally, like very much. But there are many ways of preparing fish, and if you're to serve it up to me, I would insist that it was properly presented and not suffering from lack of condiments. I'm sure a woman like Julie would feel the same.'

As for the alcohol, Frances said she was aware that her son hardly ever touched it, but modern young women expected to have a glass with their meal, and it would reflect poorly on him if he was unable to offer it. Baxter decided not to tell her that he'd already thought of this and taken care of it—what she didn't know wouldn't hurt her.

They walked together through the house to the kitchen, with Frances declaring that the place was much improved, and that she was glad after all that he hadn't knocked it down. Then, while he stored the goodies she'd brought, she exclaimed with joy over the renovated kitchen.

For dinner Baxter had stuffed a snapper with orange and herbs, and made up a plate from the local cheesemaker—he'd long been aware that his mother fancied a good slice of cheese. The meal was accompanied by an excellent white wine.

Over dinner his mother asked him how his writing was coming along, her eyebrows arched. He hoped he could brush her off with a simple answer and not get into their familiar argument about *River of Dreams*.

'I'm making some progress and I'm doing what I want to do.'

'Well,' she said, sounding prim, 'I want you to know that I still think it's a most unsavoury subject. *Must* you write about such unpleasant events?'

Here we go, Baxter thought. 'It's probably the greatest evil in our society, Mum,' he said. 'And your publisher certainly seemed interested.'

Frances sighed. 'You could write about a poor boy who rose to become a great chef with his own restaurant. You know a lot about food and how to cook it, and you wouldn't have to go near street girls.'

'What a good idea,' Baxter said lightly, although she'd already told him about it over the phone. 'Maybe that's what I'll do after I become a published author.'

'People are *very* interested in food, Greg. It's a huge industry.'

Baxter had heard this speech before too—many times. But he was relieved to be off the topic of his book, and he enjoyed watching his mother speak so passionately about her life's work, her eyes shining.

'Almost every country in the world has its unique recipes,' she continued, gesturing with her fork. 'And in France every region has its specialities—Périgord is famous for its truffles, Provence for its garlic-seasoned tomatoes. There's no end to the recipes.' Frances paused, then leaned closer to him and asked, very seriously, 'What about a murder to get hold of a famous recipe?'

'A very inventive suggestion, mother dear.'

•

After Frances had complimented him on the food, they retired to sit on the front verandah so they could contemplate the serenity of the river. Chief sat between them and watched everything.

'How old is Julie Rankin?' Frances asked, seemingly out of the blue.

'A few years younger than me, Mum. I thought you knew she was eighteen when she came to me to learn martial arts. Why?'

'I see. A lot of today's professional women are having their babies well into their late thirties. Even into their early forties, but that poses some risks.'

'What has that got to do with anything?' Baxter asked, shifting uncomfortably in his chair.

'Don't be obtuse, Greg. Women aren't like men—they can't go on forever siring children. And the older the woman is, the more chance there is of her producing children with problems.'

Baxter thought about this for a while before venturing a response. 'Julie tells me that with new medical developments, more women may be able to have babies into their late forties and early fifties.'

'What a ghastly thought!' Frances exclaimed. 'How many women would want to be rearing children at *that* age? It's too arduous. I wouldn't have wanted to deliver you at forty or older, the great lump that you were.' She smiled to show she was half-kidding.

'Professional women earning big money can afford to employ nannies, Mum. You could have done that with me—you just chose not to, and I'm grateful for it. Look, I know where you're heading. I know how much you want grandchildren, but I can't do anything to fast-forward the process.'

'Can't or won't?' Frances asked sharply.

Baxter shook his head. 'I'd marry Julie tomorrow if she said the word. But she likes me well enough as a cobber, not a lover.' He couldn't help the sadness that crept into his voice, and his mother's eyes filled with sympathy.

'Have you ever told her how you feel about her? I know you liked her a lot before she went overseas.'

'I still like her a lot, and I think being mates would be a good start to married life, but Julie won't take that last step. If I push her too hard, she might give up coming out to fish with me, and I don't want that to happen. I gave her my word that I wouldn't try anything unless she gave me the green light.'

'It's terribly frustrating. I just don't understand how she could resist you.'

'It seems she wants to do her own thing, unencumbered by a husband. She doesn't want to commit herself to a man. Any man. That's what she told me.'

Frances gave a dramatic sigh and reached out to squeeze her son's hand. 'It seems I'm no nearer to my grandchildren than I was five years ago.'

'Sorry, Mum.'

'Can you arrange for Julie to come here for a meal? I'd like to meet her again.'

'Actually, I've already invited her—she'll be over tomorrow night.'

•

Baxter reckoned that the effort Frances put into preparing dinner for Julie would be more likely to scare her away from him than attract her. She'd never be able to match his mother's expertise in the kitchen. She might feel that this was what he'd been used to and would expect from a wife, which was far from true. Baxter knew that Julie was happy to eat simple meals, and on the days she operated she ate very little.

But Baxter's gloomy predictions didn't play out—Julie was full of praise for his mother's efforts and didn't seem at all worried.

Bloody amazing, Baxter thought. *Women can be so unpredictable.*

There was also the fact that because Frances was such a dominant personality, many people were intimidated by her. But Julie was a professional used to dealing with a wide variety of people, so she wasn't at all intimidated. Like Frances, she could cut a person down to size very quickly, which meant she could be devastating with men.

Julie made a great impression. One of her secrets lay in the way she carried herself—and, of course, she was lovely. If she was deficient in anything, it was overt warmth. Julie's was a cool beauty, concealing what Baxter knew to be her fiery nature.

•

'Satisfied, Mum?' Baxter asked, when Julie's car had pulled out onto the Moondilla road.

'Quite satisfied, Greg,' Frances said, smiling broadly. 'I can understand why you're taken with her—she's a very superior person. And remember, I'm speaking as the employer of *many* young women. I pride myself on being a good judge of my sex.'

'Well, Chief likes Julie too, and I'm rapidly coming to believe that he's an excellent judge of people.' Baxter grinned at his mother. 'I might not mind if you disapproved, but if Chief objected to Julie, I'd be in a spot of bother.'

'And Julie thinks that Chief is an exceptionally clever dog,' Frances said. 'So the feeling is mutual.'

'Not much doubt about that,' he agreed.

'I agree with Julie, Greg—you've done well with that dog.'

He nodded. He'd have liked to tell her about Chief alerting him to the tiger snake on the lawn, but then she would worry about him every day of her life. She'd probably want him to return to Sydney, where the only snakes were on two legs. If Frances had the vaguest notion that his life might be in danger, whether from snakes or drug riffraff, she would never let up on him. No Greg, no grandchildren: it was as simple as that.

Baxter and his mother walked back inside the house to have a cup of coffee and some cake at the kitchen table.

'Is it really true that Julie actually puts bait on a hook?' Frances asked. 'She has beautiful hands.'

'I kid you not, Mum. That's exactly what she does. Julie can tie on two hooks to my one. She puts a cushion under her behind and sits on my jetty for a couple of hours at a time. That's when she's not fishing from my boat. I think it's her way of getting a break from the practice.'

'Now that I've met Julie I can understand your dilemma,' Frances said and sighed. 'She's not an easy fish to catch.'

170

'I wouldn't describe it as a dilemma. I'm simply letting things take their course and seeing what happens. If I press too hard, she'll slip away.' He shrugged. 'It's a bit taxing on the old bod, but I can live with that.'

'Men and their libidos,' Frances said scornfully.

Baxter chuckled. 'Don't knock it, Mum. I'll bet you drove Dad silly to get at you. If you hadn't, I wouldn't be here.'

'I must say you are the most vexing person, Greg,' she said. 'How am I to ever have any grandchildren if you veto every worthwhile young woman you meet? There were some lovely girls back in Sydney, and you found fault with every one of them.'

'In the event that Julie and I get together, I'll do my best for you, Mum,' Baxter said, a gleam in his eye.

'I'm sure you will,' Frances said, though it seemed she'd missed the real significance of her son's response. 'But if I'd had a daughter, I'm sure she would have given me grandchildren *long* ago.'

'I'm sorry to be such a disappointment to you, Mum,' Baxter said, not sure whether he felt like laughing or crying.

Frances frowned. 'Don't be absurd. Generally speaking, I'm very pleased with you. You disappoint me occasionally, but that doesn't mean I'm disappointed with you overall. Far from it. Every time I look at you, I feel well pleased that I produced you. You're what women call a hunk.'

Baxter stood, picked his mother up in his arms as if she weighed no more than a feather, and kissed her on the cheek.

'I've never been disappointed having you as my mother—and I can't think of any mother I'd prefer to have. In fact, I'd rate you as one of the best mothers going around.' He put her back on her feet and noted that she seemed genuinely pleased by what he'd said.

'If I were a young woman I should think it would be very exciting being married to you, Greg. Taxing, but exciting.'

CHAPTER TWENTY-FIVE

Baxter had a lovely time with his mother and some of her old friends around town.

The night before she was due to head back to Sydney, Frances surprised her son with a question. 'Aren't you going to take me out in your boat?'

Baxter looked at her in amazement. His mother had always professed not to like being out on the water: she'd told him that it made her ill. 'Sorry, Mum, I didn't think of doing that—I thought you hated boats.'

'Well, since you've got one, I might as well have a go. I'm not a coward, you know, and I don't like the thought that there's anything I can't do.'

'All right, but don't you want to be on the road before noon?' She'd told him that on Friday afternoon she needed to prepare for a group of VIPS, who were famous and wealthy enough to require her personal attention.

'Greg, you know I'm used to getting up at the crack of dawn.'

'Yes, but you're on holiday. Look, I'll organise everything, then come get you from the house around seven-thirty.'

•

It was a cool, bright morning, and Chief showed his usual pleasure at walking towards the water and his enemies, the ducks. However, as they drew closer to the river, for once the shepherd didn't stay close to Baxter but instead ran about in wide circles and constantly sniffed the air.

Finally he ran down to the jetty, pointed his nose at *Flora Jane*—and growled.

Baxter ran over to stand beside his dog. 'What is it, mate?'

The shepherd kept growling, clearly disturbed. Baxter looked down at the river, where *Flora* was bobbing gently on the run-in tide. She didn't look any different, and as far as Baxter knew, nothing out of the ordinary had happened to her. After the trip to the Islands, Steve Lewis had run her home and Jane had gone to Riverview and picked him up. *Flora* had been at her mooring for the few days since then.

But if Chief thought something was amiss, then as sure as blazes it was.

Had the boat been tampered with, or had something incriminating been planted on her? Baxter decided to contact

Ian Latham as soon as he could. In the meantime, he certainly wasn't taking his mother anywhere near *Flora*, but he didn't want to worry her—or to explain everything. As he hurried back, he came up with a white lie.

'Sorry, Mum, I can't oblige you this trip,' he told her, sitting down across from her at the kitchen table. 'Something's gone funny with poor *Flora*'s engine. Must've happened when I took that fishing trip to the Islands over the weekend—she had a bit of a cough by the time I got back. I'll have to get my mate Steve to take a look.'

Baxter knew his mother wouldn't ask any questions, because she was even more hopeless with mechanical things than him.

'What a pity,' she said, 'I was looking forward to a nice cruise on the river. It's such a lovely, tranquil stretch of water.' She was putting on a good show, but he could tell she was secretly relieved—a white lie to answer a white lie! 'Oh well.' She yawned and got up to make a cup of tea. 'It's quite old, isn't it?' she asked over her shoulder.

'Do you mean the river or my *Flora*?'

'The *boat*, Greg,' she said, raising her eyes heavenward.

'She's not young, but she's a decent enough runabout.'

'Well, the boat obviously has a problem, and Julie says it's a bit small for ocean fishing. Will you allow me to buy you a bigger one?'

Baxter's eyebrows lifted—his mother's generosity never failed to surprise him. Of course, he had his fingers crossed that his boat wasn't permanently damaged, and he didn't want her to waste her money. 'What's with this sudden interest you have for boats? I really thought you hated them.'

Frances nodded. 'I did. Your father took me out when I was pregnant, and I was violently ill. I thought I might lose you. It was out near the Islands and there was a big swell running. That experience put me off the water for some time, but not long ago I was taken for a lunch cruise up Middle Harbour, and I had no trouble whatsoever. This is such a quiet river that I think I'd be right as rain. Perhaps the next time I come down we'll take Julie for a cruise and have lunch somewhere?'

'That sounds great, Mum, though I'm quite happy with *Flora*. She's plenty good enough for river fishing, and we can use Steve's boat for outside trips.'

'No, I insist—for my own comfort! And we can call it a birthday present.'

Baxter sighed and gave her a fond smile. 'All right, Mum. Thanks.'

'You find the boat you like and let me know how much it is. I shall expect you to have it here next time I come down.'

'When do you reckon that will be?'

'Hopefully no more than a couple of months. In fact, how about I come down for your birthday? We'll have a small party, although this house is hardly ideal for entertaining.' She glanced around. 'Honestly, though it's much nicer than when we bought it, it *is* a tiny bit cramped, isn't it?'

Baxter felt a prickle of annoyance. 'This house suits me fine, Mum. I didn't pick it with entertaining in mind—I came here to write. And if it's a fine night, you couldn't ask for a better outdoors site. I've had lights installed and it's a magical place.'

'Yes, dear, I'm sure it is.'

'They're not cheap, you know,' he put in, not wanting to rehash their discussions about the house.

'What aren't?'

'New boats.'

'The one I was on was very nice,' Frances said. 'It had a kitchen and a bedroom *and* a shower.'

Baxter's eyes widened. 'Lord above! Were you on Packer's yacht?'

'No, nothing like that,' she said, shrugging. 'Just a nice comfortable little boat.'

'I don't need a boat like that. I'm not aiming to travel very far, or even stay out at night unless Steve and I go bream fishing.'

'A boat with a kitchen and a bedroom could be very romantic,' Frances said lightly. 'I think it would offer definite possibilities.'

The extent to which his mother was prepared to go to get him married now became very clear to him.

'You shock me, Mum. You really do.'

'Sometimes you need to push things along, darling.'

'Not with Julie Rankin, you don't. She's very much her own person.'

'Well, whatever happens, I think a new boat would be an excellent investment in your future. You seem to be keen on fishing, and a boat and fishing go together.' She paused and raised one eyebrow. 'But if you *should* invite someone to go out on a boat with you, it would be helpful to have congenial surroundings.'

'I've always recognised that you were a good businesswoman, but not that you were such a schemer.' Baxter chuckled. 'Oh well, it's your money. I'll talk to Steve and see what he has to say about what boats are on the market.'

'Thank you, Greg,' Frances said, a gleam of satisfaction in her eyes.

Baxter shook his head. His mother was the living embodiment of the fact that you never knew how a woman would behave. Just when you thought you had her sorted out, she would do something entirely contrary to your expectations. It was best not to try and out-think a woman, Baxter felt, but instead hang loose and wait for developments.

CHAPTER TWENTY-SIX

As soon as his mother's car pulled out of his drive, Baxter walked inside and put in a call to Ian Latham: 'Southern delivery for L.'

A few minutes later, Latham rang back.

'What's the problem, Greg?' the detective asked.

'Chief's behaving very strangely about my boat. He's staring at her and growling, and he loves that boat. We go out on her all the time.'

'He's a terrific dog, champ, but maybe you're taking him too seriously?'

'No, I don't think so. Chief has always been reliable—he definitely knows something's not right. I think you ought to take a look.'

'All right, I'll have someone there inside the hour. And I probably don't need to tell you this, but just in case—don't go near your boat.'

'No worries. I haven't even gone up the jetty, in case of footprints.'

'Good to hear. While I've got you on the line—I spoke to Dr Rankin, but it's good to hear things from the horse's mouth—how did your grilling go at the station?'

'Tough for a while.' Baxter gave Latham a brief rundown.

'Don't worry, Greg,' the detective said, 'it was a put-up job. The Sydney detectives didn't suspect you for a single moment. We just have to be very careful because of you-know-who at the station. We've got one of our own in on the Drew case. We reckon that Campanelli or one of his men killed Drew, but if we arrest the kingpin for that we'll blow the whole drug operation.' He added, 'I didn't tell you that, so keep it to yourself.'

'I'd like a few minutes alone with Campanelli,' Baxter said fiercely.

'We want him alive, not dead!'

'What about half and half?'

'Nix to that, champ,' Latham said tightly. 'Stay right away from Campanelli, or you might end up the next one sleeping with the fishes. We'll nail him soon enough.'

'You *hope*. What about Liz Drew? Julie says she's terrified.'

'I can understand how you feel. Just hang fire for a little

while and we should be able to put Campanelli out of circulation for quite a few years.'

'I'll believe it when I see it,' Baxter said, a chill in his voice. 'People like him always appear to have an escape alley.'

•

Baxter didn't have long to wait. A cream-coloured, half-cabin launch drifted in and tied up about fifty metres on the upriver side of Baxter's jetty, and not long after its arrival Latham's disreputable panel van pulled up beside the house.

The detective walked down to wait with Baxter and Chief beside the jetty, while his colleague—a sharp-eyed, grizzled man named Mal, whom Latham described as a forensics expert—inspected first the jetty ('No footprints!') and then the *Flora Jane*.

After only a few seconds, Mal climbed out and up onto the jetty. The grim smile on his face told Baxter that he'd been right to call Latham.

'You should give your dog a feed of steak tonight,' Mal said. 'There's a bomb inside the engine cover.'

Shocked, Baxter shot Latham a look, and saw that the detective didn't seem to share his surprise.

Mal continued, 'It's wired up to explode when the ignition is turned on, and there's enough explosive there to blow your boat to Kingdom Come. More than enough.'

'Can you defuse it?' Latham asked.

'Of course,' Mal said, looking offended. 'And do you want to try for prints, Ian?'

'I certainly do. We can't pass up the chance to nail the bugger.'

Mal nodded and headed to his launch, returning with a small case of tools. He called out to Latham, 'You've been undercover too long, mate. Get that civvie and his pup out of here!'

Latham and Baxter grinned at each other, then headed back to the house with Chief. They sat on the verandah, drinking coffee and watching Mal at work.

Baxter spoke about his suspicions. 'I reckon they wired my boat after they were told the police were letting me go. Sounds like inside information to me.'

'Yep, sounds that way. They tried to make you the number one suspect, and when that failed, they opted for the bomb. They want access to this property and they know you're out to make things as difficult for them as possible.'

Baxter's hands clenched, his knuckles white. 'I can face anyone head-on, but this underworld stuff is tough. These fellows have no ethics—they're just grubs.'

Latham nodded grimly and sipped his coffee. 'Tell me about it.'

Emerging from the boat, Mal put his fists in the air and called out, 'Victory!'

'Glad you're still in one piece,' Latham called back. He and Baxter had a chuckle and the mood lightened a little. They went down to the jetty and stood yarning while Mal attached a towrope to *Flora*.

'Until you blokes have sorted all of this out,' Baxter said, 'it looks like I'll have to stay put here with Chief. They could plant a bomb in my car next.'

'That might be the safest course for the time being,' Latham agreed. 'You and Chief ought to be able to handle anything here. Keep that old shotgun handy and your eyes skinned. And maybe you could arrange for someone to bring out your tucker.'

'I'll talk to Julie,' Baxter said. 'Assuming it's all right for her to know the story?'

'That's fine—but she's as far as it goes, all right?'

Mal gave the signal that he was ready to head off, and they called out thanks before he zoomed upriver, *Flora* swinging back and forth a little in his wake.

'We've got a shed in town,' said Latham. 'We'll go over your boat there.'

'For as long as it takes, Ian. And thanks.'

'Be seeing you, champ. You did the right thing calling me.'

When Latham had left, Baxter phoned Julie Rankin, who was quite agreeable to bringing out his meat and groceries when he told her about the bomb. In fact, she was uptight about it. He could hear she was genuinely concerned for his safety—and despite the real danger, it gave him a nice feeling to know that she was worried about him.

CHAPTER TWENTY-SEVEN

Whether it was wet or fine, Baxter always took Chief for a final romp around the house before he went to bed. Baxter had wet-weather gear, of course, and Chief had a raincoat so that he didn't bring too much wet into the house.

It wasn't raining this night. The moon was out, with the river a long stretch of polished silver. Somewhere far away, a mopoke was repeating its monotonous call.

Baxter was strolling towards the big shrubs with Chief just behind him. Out of the silence, the dog growled.

Baxter didn't wait. He leapt sideways, performed a standing jump of three metres and followed it up with a lightning-fast somersault that brought him to his feet. Two men stepped out from behind a camellia, carrying what appeared to be iron bars.

One glance was all it took for Baxter to weigh up the situation. An iron bar could break an arm or paralyse it, while a hit to the head could knock a man out—or kill a dog. One man with an iron bar was bad enough, but two was more than even Baxter and Chief could handle. The only solution was to separate the men so he could deal with them one at a time.

Signalling Chief to stay still and silent, Baxter sprinted for the closest shed, guessing that one man would follow while the other ran to block him. Then he ducked beside the shed and put out a leg to trip his follower. He hit him once very hard, and the man went down and stayed down.

Baxter picked up the man's iron bar and turned as the other man came around the corner of the shed. He pulled up when he saw Baxter with the bar, the large German Shepherd running to stand beside him, and his partner flat out on the ground.

'Put the bar down, buster, you're out of your league,' Baxter said harshly. 'I learned this game from the people who invented it.'

Chief gave a loud bark.

The man backed away and, when he was clear of the shed, looked to the jetty.

'Got someone there, have you?' Baxter asked. 'Who sent you . . . Campanelli?'

There was a shot—very loud in the silence of the night—and the man staggered and then fell. The shot was followed by the sound of a boat engine starting up.

'Watch him, Chief,' Baxter commanded as he ran for the jetty. He could see the small boat out on the silver water, but not well enough to identify it.

Baxter retraced his steps and stopped beside the badly wounded man. He tried to give him first aid, but it was clear he wouldn't last long.

'I don't think much of the company you keep, buster,' Baxter said. 'You might not be up to much, but getting shot in the back is a poor way to die. Was it Campanelli?'

'Camp—' the man gurgled, and then he died.

Baxter walked to where the other fellow was still out cold. He made him as comfortable as possible. 'Keep watching him, Chief.'

After phoning for an ambulance, Baxter put in a call for Latham. 'Don't touch anything, champ,' the detective said. 'I'll have a team there as soon as possible.'

Inside the hour there was a flotilla of vehicles at Riverview. Julie came with the ambulance in her capacity as medical examiner. She said that the downed man was in a coma and there was no telling how long he'd remain in this condition.

'Are you all right, Greg?' she asked, her forehead creased with concern.

'Yes, they didn't touch me. Once I'd split them up, I knew I could handle them.'

'The big question is whether that shot was meant for your trespasser or for you,' Latham said. 'Maybe the Big Chief who runs this racket doesn't like loose ends.'

'All I got out of him was "Camp—", and then he died.'

'Better him than you.' Latham's smile was thin. 'You're going to cost me a lot of money, Greg. I'm going to mount a watch over you and this place—'

'Is that really necessary?' Baxter asked, while Julie exclaimed, 'Good idea!'

'—until we have Campanelli behind bars,' Latham finished. 'You and Chief clearly make a great team, but I've decided it would be irresponsible of me not to give you some back-up. I've asked my superiors and they've come up with the funds.'

After providing his official statement and saying goodnight, Baxter started walking back to the house past Mal and a few other overall-clad forensics officers.

'Anything worthwhile?' he asked Mal.

'Not much so far, but we haven't checked the bars for fingerprints.'

'You'll find mine on one of them—I didn't touch the other.'

CHAPTER TWENTY-EIGHT

A concerned Liz Drew rang early the next morning—Julie had relayed some of the night's proceedings.

'I'm fine, Liz,' he said. 'Not a scratch on me.'

'You're amazing, in other words. Any other man would have fallen to pieces. But aren't you still in danger?'

Once Baxter had reassured Liz as much as he could, she asked, 'Can I come out and see you, Greg? I want some advice and I trust you more than anyone else.'

'All right, Liz. Come round now and we'll have a cup of tea.'

He could see that the day was going to be a non-event for his writing, because Julie had told him the night before that she'd be heading over for lunch. Two female visitors in one day—his mother would have been thrilled.

•

In her smart new blue jeans and a cream blouse, Liz looked terrific, but her eyes were tired. She'd been up to Riverview only once before—just quickly to pick up her car—and this time she gave both the property and Chief quite a few compliments.

Baxter made a pot of tea and they sat out on the verandah in the usual spot.

'I need to know whether you think I'm doing the right thing,' she said nervously, tucking a strand of loose blonde hair behind her ear.

'What do you mean?'

'I'm planning to sell my house and go back to my property in Queensland.'

'Ah, right.' He was surprised by the surge of disappointment he felt at the idea of her leaving.

'The thing is, I'll never feel safe here while Campanelli is on the loose. He could send a couple of his men for me, and once I'm on his yacht anything could happen.'

Her hands were shaking so much that she had to set down her tea.

'Are you sleeping, Liz?' Baxter asked.

'Julie's given me sleeping pills, but they've got their problems too. I don't want to be too out to it, in case I don't hear Campanelli's men coming for me.' She put her face in her hands. 'Do you think I'm doing the right thing by selling up and running away?'

'Please don't think of it like that—it's a sensible plan.'

Liz reached out a trembling hand and he took it, giving it a gentle squeeze.

'In the meantime,' he said, 'I'd get a security mob to fix up all your windows and doors, and maybe install an alarm. It might cost a few bob but it would give you great peace of mind.'

'I'd thought of that—Jack left me a few thousand—but I don't know who to trust around town. Except you and Julie, of course.'

'I reckon Steve Lewis at Moondilla Motors could do it for you, or give you a recommendation. Julie and I trust him, so you can too.'

Liz turned tear-filled eyes on Baxter, her hand still warm in his. 'All right.'

'Immediately, Liz.'

Just then, Chief gave the bark that let his master know someone was coming up the drive. Baxter walked around and saw it was Julie, running a little early.

•

If Julie was piqued to find Liz with Baxter—and he hoped she was—she managed to hide it very well.

For lunch he served the women corned beef, creamy mashed potatoes and salad, followed by rhubarb pie and cream. The three of them chatted about everything but the dire situation in Moondilla, with Julie and Baxter making a particular effort to keep the mood light. By the time Liz headed off, she seemed a lot more relaxed.

Then Julie turned to Baxter, her eyes serious. 'Greg . . .'

'What?'

'You might consider going back to live with your mother in Sydney until Ian gets on top of this drug business.'

Baxter tensed. 'I've never run from anyone in my life.'

Looking pained, Julie got up from the table and walked over to the window, staring out with her back to him. 'You're the only man I feel anything for, and I don't want to lose you.' He could tell how much it cost her to admit that.

'But you don't want to marry me?'

She turned to give him a warning look. 'Remember your promise not to try anything, Greg.'

They stared at each other until Baxter looked away.

'What's with the fellow I dropped?' he asked. 'Still in a coma?'

'Yes, with a police guard.' Julie's voice had turned professional. 'He could be out for days, weeks or months—or he might not recover at all.'

'The police will be crooked on me for causing them to use up valuable resources.'

'I doubt that very much,' she said, her expression softening. 'Well, I'd better head back to the clinic.' She picked up her handbag. 'Thanks for the bonzer lunch. You know, a sandwich would have been enough today.'

'My mother would never forgive me if I gave you a sandwich.'

Julie grinned, her true warmth breaking through. 'Nothing wrong with a good sandwich, especially if it's multigrain bread.'

CHAPTER TWENTY-NINE

On one of his long evening walks with Chief, Baxter decided to head across to the old dairy building. This dated back to Riverview's origin as a dairy farm with a noted Jersey herd. When the farm had been subdivided, decades ago, Harry Carpenter—who'd married the daughter of the adjoining dairy farmer—had acquired fifty acres.

The old dairy building was still quite sound, with a solid concrete floor and its roof in fair condition. Possums played in the building at night, and it was occasionally visited by a masked owl in search of mice.

Baxter climbed the small rise between his house and the dairy building. From this vantage spot he scanned the river and the surrounding countryside with his binoculars. There was another jetty farther upriver that he picked up clearly, but he couldn't see a single boat out on the water—well, not unusual for this time of night.

He left the rise and walked across the paddock towards the old building. He'd inspected it a couple of times and had been pondering how he could utilise it. He decided to take another look, but Chief's low growl checked him.

Baxter stiffened. He knew for certain now that Chief never growled for nothing. The shepherd was infallible. Baxter looked at his dog, whose eyes were fixed on the old dairy. 'Steady, Chief,' he muttered under his breath.

The dairy was divided in two: a long room where the cows had been milked, and an adjoining room where the milk had been treated and stored in big vats. When Baxter stepped into this room, he saw that someone had been using it—a swag, a portable stove and a lamp sat in one corner, and the windows had been bagged over.

Chief growled again, louder now, as a tall, dark-haired man stepped through from the other room. He put up his hand and smiled reassuringly. 'It's okay, Mr Baxter. I'm with Ian Latham. The name's Lester. Tell your dog I'm on your side.'

Lester was dressed in dark jeans and a khaki shirt, and he too was carrying binoculars. Baxter took him to be a fellow not much older than himself.

'It's okay, Chief,' Baxter said, rubbing his dog's ears. 'So you're the one keeping watch over me?' he asked Lester.

'That and other things. And there's two of us—we take it in shifts. Ian reckoned you wouldn't mind us using the old dairy.'

'It's all right, though I would've preferred to be kept in the loop. So what's doing?'

'Things are finally coming to a head.' He sounded optimistic. 'We reckon they'll transfer the big drug shipment in three or four days. What we don't know is where they'll drop it. We do know that it won't be at your place, and now we're thinking it may not be anywhere along the river.'

'I noticed there's a jetty farther along.'

'Don't worry, we've got them all pinpointed. The road in to that one is bad—virtually unusable in wet weather.'

Baxter nodded, relieved. 'But have they got anyone watching my place?'

'Not that we know of, and I doubt they could do it under our noses. But there's other things on their minds right now . . . like several million dollars' worth of drugs.'

'I hope you can keep those bastards from getting their hands on a cent.'

Lester grinned. 'That's the idea.'

'You need anything?' Baxter asked, casting his eyes around the room again. 'This is a pretty rough camp.'

'It goes with the job,' Lester said and smiled thinly. 'I'll manage. I don't expect to be here much longer.'

'You could always come to the house and I'd cook you a decent meal.'

'Thanks, but you can't watch things from inside a house. Ian would have my hide if I slipped up on this job. We hope to put Campanelli away for a good long stretch.'

'That's a worthy goal, but he and his ilk exert influence even from inside prison.'

'True enough. The Mr Bigs are a constant concern for us, and the lure of big money will always ensure that there are Mr Bigs. But we do what we can.'

'Too right. And I appreciate you looking out for me.' Baxter glanced at his watch. 'I'd better be getting back. Ian calls me every night.' He grinned fondly. 'He can be a bit of a mother hen, but he's all right.'

'He's a top man,' Lester said with an answering grin. 'One of the best. And you know, he's got a personal stake in the drug business.'

'What's that?' Baxter couldn't remember Latham mentioning anything.

'He might not like me telling you this, but I think it'll help you fully trust him. When he was a boy, his older brother died from an overdose. It nearly killed Ian's parents. Cost them their marriage, too. So Ian's real crooked on drug pushers.'

Another tragedy caused by the rotten stuff. Baxter felt sick to his stomach. 'How awful. What a great bloke he is to be taking them on like this. And of course I'll keep it in confidence—no worries on that score.'

So many lives lost to drugs: Julie and Jane's brother, Andrew. Rosa. The undercover policewoman and her sister. Latham's brother. Then there were the lives of their loved ones, forever marred by their deaths.

Just as Baxter was about to say his goodbyes and go, he turned back.

'Something else worrying you?' Lester asked.

'Did they do any good with my boat? I mean, did they lift any fingerprints?'

'One good set. They belong to Yat Lee, one of Campanelli's hoods.' Lester crooked a smile. 'He wasn't too careful. I suppose he reckoned that when the boat blew up, there wouldn't be any fingerprints to lift. So we now have clear evidence of his involvement in a crime, and it's unlikely he can slip through our net, whatever happens.'

'Yat Lee, eh. I'll remember that name,' Baxter said grimly. He looked forward to the day when he could meet up with this creep.

'He's a bad egg, Mr Baxter.'

'Aren't they all?'

'No, really,' Lester insisted. 'If you meet up with him, don't give him any slack. He'd shoot or knife you and not think twice about it.'

Baxter nodded. 'I'll bear that in mind.' As he walked out the door, Chief at his heels, he said, 'When this is all over, you should come and have a meal with me.'

'I'll keep you to that. See ya, mate.'

Walking back to the house over the lush paddocks of mixed grasses, Baxter took deep breaths of the fresh night air. It felt very strange that a member of a massive police investigation was living in Riverview's old dairy.

Baxter remembered Latham's words: *You're going to cost me a lot of money, Greg.* That made him think about what it was costing taxpayers to try and control the drug problem. It seemed no matter how much effort the authorities devoted to drugs, they would never eliminate them. Human inventiveness knew no limits, and Australia's vast coastline made things even more difficult.

But this time, at least, the police appeared to have the upper hand. That creep Yat Lee had incriminated himself, and he and Campanelli and all of their associates would soon be going down.

CHAPTER THIRTY

Between six and seven a few evenings later, Baxter was fishing from his jetty. In case someone managed to get past Lester and take a shot at him, he wasn't sitting right on top but on the loading ramp to one side—he didn't feel in danger, though. The sun was going down behind the mountain range to the west, and everything was very quiet along the river. It was the best time of the day for fishing, and Baxter had two good flathead in his sugar bag, tied to a pylon.

Chief was lying quietly behind him. The shepherd was exhausted after a day of excitement—Steve Lewis had come by around noon and dropped off Baxter's magnificent new boat. Chief had run aboard, barking excitedly at all the new smells. She was now tethered to the jetty, gleaming in the fading sunlight. Baxter hadn't decided what to call her yet. He knew it was sentimental, but he missed old *Flora Jane*.

Presently, Chief growled, stood up and pointed his nose towards the track that led down to the main road. 'Surely not someone at this hour,' Baxter muttered.

He stood up as a car pulled to a stop beside the house. Then his eyes widened when Liz Drew got out and came walking down to the jetty. She lifted her hand in a wave, which he returned. Immediately his annoyance left him. He wound up his handline and went to meet her.

'Hi, Greg,' Liz said as he came up close to her. She gave him a dazzling smile, put her arms around his neck, and then kissed him warmly on the cheek.

'This is an unexpected pleasure, Liz,' Baxter said, stepping back and scrutinising her. 'You look very well.'

She was dressed in blue jeans and a red blouse, and wore a grey Akubra pushed back on her head. She looked about eighteen. For a moment Baxter had a picture of her as he reckoned she might have looked when she first came to Moondilla with the country and western troupe.

'Thank you. I feel well, too. I'm going home, Greg. *Home*. Back to the cattle property Dad left me.' She beamed. 'I sold my house and I'm packed and on my way. Can I stay here with you tonight?'

Baxter looked at her. What Liz wanted didn't have to be spelt out.

His heart leapt. 'If that's what you want,' he said.

She didn't say anything—she just smiled.

Baxter walked back along the jetty and stowed his handline in his fishing basket. He pulled the sugar bag out of the river, untied it from the pylon and let the water drain from it. As he worked, he cast a glance in the direction of the old dairy, wondering what Lester or the other bloke was thinking of all this.

When Baxter re-joined Liz, she took his arm and they walked up to the house. He paused beside her car and smiled—it was packed to the roof with boxes and suitcases. A guitar case lay on top of the pile.

'You really are going home,' he said.

'I really am.' She sighed, then she shot him a wicked look. 'But not yet.'

He laughed. 'Let me carry your bag, Liz.'

She dug about among the cases on the front seat and came up with a small overnight bag. 'That's all I'll need tonight,' she said, and they went up to the verandah, his arm still in hers. Chief was walking beside them, and Liz looked at him and shook her head. 'I'd like a dog same as Chief. Would there be one, I wonder?'

'Maybe, maybe not, but I think he's exceptional. If I own other dogs they'll all have to stand comparison to him. He's a fantastic mate and a tremendous watchdog.'

'Well, Chief is going to have to share you with me tonight,' Liz said. They walked inside. 'Where's your bedroom?'

He grinned. 'Down the hall and to the left—if you're sure that's what you want.'

Liz stopped and dropped one hand to a well-shaped hip. 'Don't you?'

The look in his eyes gave her the answer, and she smiled and turned away.

•

When she came out of the bedroom, he asked if she'd like a drink.

'A gin and tonic would be nice, if you run to such things. I mean, I know you don't drink. Orange juice would be fine too.'

'Mum brought me some drinks on her last visit. She thinks its inhospitable not to have an array on hand for visitors, especially for—in her words—modern young women who expect such things.'

'Some mother,' Liz said, laughing.

'You can say that again. Did you notice my new boat?'

'The one tied to the jetty? It looked very impressive.'

'Well, it's an early birthday present from Mum.'

'Some present!'

He fixed Liz's drink and handed it to her. 'I'm off to the kitchen now. Would you like to have a shower or watch some TV while I cook?'

'I'd prefer to watch *you*,' Liz said and smiled.

Liz's smile was something else, Baxter thought. It promised a lot—a hell of a lot.

She followed him into the kitchen, perched herself on a stool, and watched him while she sipped her gin and tonic. 'Tell me if I can help,' she asked after a little while.

'Thanks. You can take some plates and cutlery from these cupboards and set the table. There's tablecloths in the drawer beside you.'

'That all?' she asked and laid a hand on his arm.

'For now,' he said, his voice low.

She smiled and followed his instructions. 'What are you preparing?' she asked when she returned to the kitchen.

'A bit of this and a bit of that,' he answered. 'I hope you like it.'

'You couldn't do anything I wouldn't like.'

'You'll give me a big head, Liz.'

'Well, after that lunch you made last time, I have an idea of what you can do in the kitchen. And Julie keeps me informed about your other culinary masterpieces. Isn't *she* the lucky one?' Liz arched an eyebrow.

Baxter didn't want to talk about Julie—not tonight, anyway. 'Mum taught me to appreciate food. She says that every meal should taste good enough to be remembered long afterwards.'

There was a gleam in Liz's eyes. 'That's true of so many things.'

•

Later, after complimenting him on the meal, Liz insisted on doing the washing up. She did it hastily: apparently she didn't wish to dwell in the kitchen. As Baxter was putting things away, her hand rested lightly on his backside. Heat surged through his body.

'What now, Greg?' she asked.

'I'm going to have a bath—I probably smell a bit fishy.'

'All right, but you smell pretty good to me.'

He was soaking in the bath when she appeared in the doorway, just as he'd hoped. She walked to the side of the tub and looked down at him.

'My God,' she breathed.

He watched her unbutton her blouse and place it across the bathroom chair. It was followed by her bra and then her jeans and knickers. Free of her clothes, she stepped into the bath and sat down behind him. She bent forward and kissed him.

He leaned back against her and felt her lovely breasts pressing against his back. She was soaping and kissing him simultaneously. 'You sure have a great body,' she said.

'So have you,' he said, and leaned his head against hers.

'It's not quite what it was.'

'No, I'm sure it's even better.'

She laughed softly and put her hand to his groin. 'You ready to get out?'

He stepped out of the tub, then gave her his hand and watched her as she stood up. He handed her a big fluffy towel and she rubbed herself dry with slow, provocative movements. When she'd finished, she walked to the bathroom

door and looked back at him. Every movement she made was
unforgettable.

'You won't be long, will you?' she asked.

'I'll be right behind you, Liz.'

She nodded, smiled and then swayed away. She was
completely at home in her nakedness.

•

Liz was lying on the bed when Baxter walked into his room.
Her lovely body was outlined against the deep blue silk sheets
his mother had insisted on buying him, and her long blonde
hair was spread like a halo across a blue pillow. She put her
arms up to him. 'Come here, you black belt maestro, and show
me how you perform in bed.'

A grey shape jumped up onto the foot of the bed and
then made its way towards the pillows. Baxter watched in
amusement as Chief put his head down and licked Liz on the
face before retreating back down the bed.

'That's a first,' she said, laughing. 'I've never been to bed
with a man and his dog.'

Baxter was laughing too. 'Chief's just given you his seal of
approval, Liz. He'll get down when I get in. He always sleeps
on the floor beside me.'

When Baxter climbed in beside Liz, sure enough Chief
jumped off the bed and lay beside it. 'What a dog,' Liz breathed
as she reached for Baxter.

'What a woman,' he said and kissed her.

He was to remember this night for a long time. He'd slept with a few women, all of them younger and some of them fitter than Liz, but none had come near her in bed. While they'd given him some memorable experiences, Liz eclipsed every one of them.

CHAPTER THIRTY-ONE

Baxter didn't get much sleep that night and was feeling very light-headed when he got up the next morning. Liz was sound asleep with a half-smile on her face.

No wonder, he thought, that Jack Drew had been jealous if any man even looked at Liz. She was a sexual treasure.

After having a shower and getting dressed, Baxter ate an omelette, then made another, filled a glass with orange juice and took breakfast in to his guest. She was still asleep and he hated waking her. He knew he should let her sleep on, but she had a big drive ahead of her.

'Liz,' he whispered and kissed her cheek.

'What is it, honey?' she asked and reached for him.

'Breakfast,' he said softly.

'Already?' She opened one eye and looked at the tray in his hands. 'Breakfast in bed—I've never had breakfast in bed. I want to kiss you, Greg.' She kissed him several times, then took the tray. 'Feel better, honey?'

'Considerably.' It wasn't the total truth, as he felt like going back to bed with her, but he did feel less tense.

'Think you'll remember me?' she asked, her lips brushing his cheek.

'For a very long time,' he assured her. 'Go on, have some breakfast. You should be ready for it after last night.'

•

He was reading a two-day-old newspaper when she came into the kitchen, freshly showered and wearing the same blue jeans but with a different blouse. There was a real glow about her that he thought was pretty incredible, considering the effort she'd expended during the night.

'You look good enough to eat,' he said. 'Tea or coffee?' The two pots were sitting in front of him on the table.

'Coffee would be wonderful,' she said, sitting down.

He poured her a mug and then appraised her again. 'You shouldn't look as good as you do,' he said.

She shrugged and gave him a small, pleased smile. 'I was feeling very fresh last night. You know, I'd been thinking about you quite a lot.'

The idea of her thinking about him like that made him hot all over. 'I'm not sure exactly how to put this, Liz, but you're the most . . . the most *woman* I've ever known. I hope you understand what I mean.'

'I like sex,' she said, matter-of-fact. 'Especially when it's with someone I really like. And I like you a lot, honey,' she added warmly.

They smiled at each other for a moment.

'What are you going to do with your life, Liz?'

She dropped her eyes and shrugged. 'Who knows, I might marry a cattleman.'

'Lucky cattleman,' he said.

She got up and came around the table to him. He felt her firm breasts press against him as she kissed him and sat on his lap. 'You can make a person feel real good without even trying,' she said huskily, and they kissed for a while, his arms around her.

When they came up for air, Baxter stroked her cheek and said, 'Don't just marry any cattleman, Liz. Marry a fellow who loves you and doesn't booze. Have a couple of kids. You're a very warm person—you'd give your kids plenty of love and affection.'

'I'll see what I can do.' She smiled down at him affectionately, then slid from his lap and sat at the table again. 'Someday I'll make a trip back here to see you and Julie. Though I should hope that there'll be no Franco Campanelli to concern me.'

'By then I'm sure there won't be,' Baxter said, thinking of what Lester had told him. 'Maybe you'll be able to bring your family.'

'Maybe.' She finished her coffee. 'There are two favours I'd like to ask of you before I go, Greg.'

'Ask away, Liz,' he said with a smile.

'I'd like you to take me for a run in your new boat. I want to remember you and this river and my last morning here.'

'Okay, what's the other?' he asked.

'I'd like to watch you doing your exercises and martial arts routines—Julie says they're worth seeing.'

'No problem,' he said. 'But when do you plan on leaving?'

She met his eyes and smiled. 'If it were only up to me I wouldn't leave at all. But, as it is . . . probably after lunch.'

•

Baxter packed ham-and-tomato sandwiches, small cream cakes and a thermos of hot water. With Liz holding on to his arm, they walked down to the jetty.

He handed her into the new boat and watched as Chief followed. Then he untied the two mooring ropes, threw them onto the boat and jumped on board. Liz stood beside him while he started the engine and listened as it purred into life.

He backed the boat out into the river and then pointed it down towards the harbour. They passed under the bridge and traversed the harbour's mouth before coming back into the river proper. When they reached the bridge again, Baxter kellicked the boat and they had their morning smoko in the cabin.

'This and what happened last night must be as close to

paradise as I'll ever experience,' Liz said and pressed his arm. 'And doesn't Chief like to be here?'

The dog's tail was wagging and he was sniffing around, his eyes bright.

'He's nuts on this boat,' Baxter agreed. 'Must be all the new smells—he has a very acute nose.'

Liz was staring out across the water, her eyes suddenly sad. 'Jack liked his boat. He was liking it more and more towards the end. If only he hadn't been so keen on the booze.' She sighed. 'I still don't understand why.'

Baxter gave her a sympathetic look. 'Neither do I. There's no answers in a bottle, Liz. Like there's no answers from using drugs.'

•

Liz sat on a chair in the shed and watched Baxter perform some of his old gymnastic exercises followed by his martial arts routine. He was clad only in white shorts and white gym shoes. When he'd finished, she told him it was a performance she was likely never to forget. She said, a sparkle in her eyes, that Baxter had the best body she'd ever seen, and she had never seen anyone who could move like him. She didn't have to add that this included her late husband.

After they'd eaten lunch, Liz handed Baxter a small slip of paper. 'That's my address and phone number in Queensland. If you'd ever like to come and visit me, you'd be more than welcome. And would you mind if I ring you occasionally?'

'You can ring me any old time,' Baxter said.

She smiled and he thought she looked young and wonderful. 'Can we talk frankly, Greg?' she asked.

He raised his eyebrows. 'I think so, Liz.'

'Your illustrious mother would probably say that I wasn't good enough for you, but if the writing business doesn't work out and you don't want to go back to cooking, I'd be very happy for you to come help me run the property.'

Smiling, he shook his head. 'I don't know the first thing about cattle, except how to cook the meat. And I thought you said you might marry a cattleman?'

'Oh, you know I was just joking. After you, any man would be a letdown, and I don't want to settle for second best. I had one bash at that.'

'There must be plenty of good men looking for good women like you.'

'I doubt I'd qualify as a good woman anymore. And from my experience, really good men are hard to find.' Her eyes were sad. 'Anyway, I want you to know that if things get tough, come to me. It's a big property—big enough to keep us.'

He wished he didn't have to hurt her, but he didn't want to give her false hope either. He took her hand, met her gaze and spoke as gently as possible. 'Look, I appreciate your offer no end, but I don't see us settling down together. And right now, all I'm interested in is my writing.'

'But you're sweet on Julie, aren't you?' Liz asked, her voice sharpening. She slid her hand from his.

'Yes, I like her a lot,' he said softly. 'I've always liked her. But Julie doesn't want a man in her life. We're good mates and that's about it.'

Liz nodded, seeming to accept this. 'I used to think she was the smartest person in Moondilla, but if she was she'd have grabbed you, Greg. A woman with any real feeling in her couldn't keep coming out here and not make love.' Liz paused, bit her lip, and said, 'Do you know she's never been to bed with a man?'

Baxter wondered if Julie would have wanted Liz to tell him that. 'You appear to know more about that side of her than I do,' he said.

'We've talked quite often, sometimes about men. I don't think you'd be happy with her, Greg. She's married to medicine.'

Liz sounded a little sharp again, but he accepted that what she'd said was probably true. It was also true that as a sexual being, Liz Drew left Julie Rankin for dead. Liz invested everything she did with her own innate appeal. A woman could work at developing a persona, and many did, but Baxter reckoned she'd been born with hers. If a fellow simply wanted a good sex life, she'd fit the bill to perfection—and of course, there was much more to Liz than her talent in the bedroom.

Baxter wondered why it was that although he felt very warmly about Liz, he didn't love her. There was a wide gulf between warmth for a woman and love. It was demonstrated by the fact that he wasn't greatly concerned about her leaving

Moondilla. If he'd loved her, he would have fought tooth and nail to keep her close to him.

There was a rumble of thunder and it began to rain. The river was pockmarked by solid droplets.

Liz got up and went to the window. 'It's going to be a wet afternoon,' she said.

'You don't have to head off in a storm. You can stay another night.'

'You don't understand. The longer I stay with you, the longer I'll want to stay and the harder it will be to leave.' But Liz made no move to get going. Instead she asked, 'While it's raining, though, can I have a look through your house?'

'Be my guest.'

'I am your guest,' she said with a smile.

She wandered with him from room to room until she found his study, which it appeared had been her objective. 'Is this where you work? Is that the book?' She pointed to where the pages of his manuscript were stacked up.

'That's it,' he said. 'Or the first draft, at least.' He sat on the edge of his big wooden desk and looked up at her. 'I've been held up because I don't know how to finish the damned thing. Beginning it was easy—it's the ending that's difficult.'

'Endings are always difficult, Greg,' she said. 'Like leaving here and you.'

He sighed and gestured to the manuscript. 'I'm going to scrap what I've done and start again.'

'You're going to scrap all that work?' she exclaimed.

'More or less. I'm going to reshape the story's direction. It's not good enough, and when I began to write it I hadn't met you or reconnected with Julie. You've inspired me.'

He wanted to write about them as well as Rosa—three very different women who'd all had their lives changed by the drug trade.

Liz looked pleased. 'And has this book got a title?'

'Nothing set in concrete, but I think of it as *River of Dreams.*'

She rolled the title over her tongue. 'I like the sound of it. I suppose living here, you can't help writing about the river.'

'That's partly right. The lovely old river out there was one of the main reasons I bought this place. But there are other meanings behind the title. A river is a source of life because so much depends on its flow, but it isn't dangerous like the ocean. And life itself is like a river. It flows on and on, then eventually it comes to an end. Our dreams form part of that flow of life.'

'That's beautiful,' Liz said. 'I'd read it based on that alone. Send me a copy?'

He grinned. 'I might even bring you one if it ever gets published.'

CHAPTER THIRTY-TWO

The rain continued to bucket down, so Baxter made a pot of tea. They sat in the living room, Liz curled up beside him on the couch.

'You didn't move to Moondilla just to write, did you?' she said.

'No, I was looking for a place that offered me an escape from Sydney . . . a kind of haven. It was an illusion that Campanelli shattered. But without dreams, life is a humdrum affair, isn't it? And at least it's better here than in Sydney. I couldn't leave the river now and go back there.'

'I had a lot of dreams. One was that I should meet a man just like you—although I never imagined he'd be a martial arts champion!' She laughed. 'That dream came to me after it was clear I wasn't going to be a country and western star. And for a long time, looking for a bonzer man proved an illusion too.'

'Tell me the story, Liz—about you and Jack.'

She nodded slowly. 'All right. When I realised I wasn't going to make it big, I was disappointed. I misbehaved and drank too much for a while myself. I decided to quit singing and stay in Moondilla—that was when I took Jack on.'

Baxter couldn't help his grimace. He wished it hadn't been like that for her.

'What was I to do, Greg? Drag around the country for years, backing the stars and staying at hundreds of motels and hotels, with men groping me at every second one of them? No star billing, no big money.' Her whole body had tensed up and her face had gone pale. 'But that's not the whole story. Early on, when I was still in the troupe, Campanelli and his men surrounded me after a concert, when I'd had a few drinks, and hustled me onto his yacht.'

Baxter looked at her in horror. 'Liz—'

'Don't worry, I was only out there for a few minutes. I was tiddly enough to think I could swim to shore, so while the yacht was still driving I pretended to trip over my own feet and fall into the water. Jack and a mate were out fishing late at the wharf. Back then he could swim like a fish, so he dived in, got me out and carried me to my hotel.'

'And then you fell for him.'

'Not completely. Jack said he needed me and he offered me a home. I wasn't aware how big a boozer he was until after I married him, but from what I could see, all men drank anyway. They all drank and they all played around.'

'Not all men play around,' Baxter said, hating the jaded note in her voice.

'You know that for a fact, do you?'

'I'm sure my father didn't—and I wouldn't.'

'I'm talking about your average male, not supermen,' she scoffed.

'I'm no superman. And if I were lucky enough to be married to a woman I loved, I certainly wouldn't cheat on her.'

Liz's eyes were damp. 'Yeah, I reckon you wouldn't.'

Baxter stroked her hair and they sat in silence for a moment.

'Well,' Liz said briskly, 'now I've found my man but he doesn't love me, so I'm going home to do something else with my life.'

She moved away from him, sitting up on the couch, and told him a little about her plans for the cattle station. She sounded full of enthusiasm as she talked about installing a feedlot and breeding cattle, things that he knew almost nothing about.

'I know you'll succeed,' he said and smiled. 'You'll have a marvellous life out there. I hope you'll find your cattleman husband and have a couple of kids too.'

She gave him a soft look of gratitude. 'You amaze me, Greg. You should know you're a wonderful man with a woman. Heaps of women would live with you in any kind of circumstance—it doesn't matter if you don't get your book published.'

'I'm not sure about that. A lot of women would try to change me because I'm not a high-flyer. Sure, I always set out to do the best I can in anything I try, but I'm a man who simply wants a peaceful, decent life.'

'I'd live with you in a tent, Greg,' Liz said. Her eyes were damp.

It had stopped raining a while before, and in the silence between them was the sound of water dripping from the roof and the trees.

'If you're going,' Baxter said, 'you'd better go, unless you've changed your mind and want to stay another night.' He took her hand and held it to his heart. 'I'll remember you and last night for a long time, Liz.'

She looked up at him, blinking her tear-filled eyes. Tears were running down her cheeks. 'I wanted this a lot, Greg. Most of all, I want to remember you in this place. You and your dog and this last morning on the river—your river of dreams.' She sniffed and wiped at her eyes. 'Now I'd better head off before I bawl my eyes out and leave you with a dreadful picture of me.'

•

The air was cooler now that the rain had ceased. Baxter carried her bag out to the car. Liz turned, put her arms around his neck and then kissed him several times: full-on kisses that would linger in his mind. Then she crouched down and put her arms around Chief's neck. 'Look after him, big dog,' she said.

'There's some very weird people travelling that northern road,' Baxter said, 'so don't pick up any hitchhikers. And ring me when you get there—I'll worry until I hear from you.'

Liz gestured to her fully packed car and grinned. 'I couldn't possibly fit in a hitchhiker even if I wanted to, but I love your concern.'

As Baxter opened the car door, Chief padded along to stand beside his master and quietly gaze up at Liz while she got in. When she turned on the ignition, she gave Baxter a look that said she could hardly bear to leave them. Then she was driving away.

Baxter stood with light rain falling on him from a transient filmy cloud that would soon pass. The cloud was like most of the best moments of his life that had passed all too quickly. He would never forget the sight of Liz lying naked on his bed, her lovely body creamy white against the blue sheets and her arms outstretched to clasp him to her. And then there was the completely uninhibited way she made love, giving everything she had to give.

If he had lifted a finger, Liz would have stayed with him— but for all she had to offer, she wasn't Julie.

CHAPTER THIRTY-THREE

It was tough going back to writing after Liz Drew's visit. The thought of her teamed up with another man like Jack worried Baxter a lot, and preoccupied him for the next few weeks. But his thoughts of Liz were interrupted by the arrival of Detective Sergeant Ian Latham.

Latham's long hair had been cut short, and he was in clean slacks and a pressed shirt. The disreputable putty-coloured van had been replaced by a white Holden.

'You almost had me thinking you were a stranger,' Baxter said, greeting Latham at his front door. 'Off the undercover work for a while?'

'Yes, thank goodness. I've got a lot of leave owing to me. And it's good to see you, Greg.' Latham shook hands with Baxter.

'What brings you here, Ian?' Baxter asked, gesturing for him to come inside.

'Some good news, for the time being at least,' Latham said, sitting down.

'Good news is never hard to take.'

Baxter had just made some coffee, so he brought two steaming mugs from the kitchen. He was hoping to hear that Campanelli had finally been arrested and the drug shipment seized.

Instead Latham said, 'It looks like Campanelli and Company have switched their field of operation. We believe they're landing drugs in Western Australia for the moment. It's a bigger hassle for them, because they have to move the stuff over vast distances, either by road or by air.'

'Then why are they doing it?'

'It's all a ploy to distract us from keeping watch here. They'll come back to Moondilla when they think we've relaxed our vigilance.'

'How do you know all this?' Baxter asked.

'We've managed to infiltrate their system. In simple terms, we've got an undercover cop in Campanelli's outfit. It's taken some doing, but he's there and he's passed us some very interesting information.'

'Sounds dangerous, especially after what happened to that policewoman.'

'Yes, it's damned risky, and it takes a bloody good cop to do it.'

Baxter nodded. 'And am I still being babysat by your blokes at the dairy, or do you think I can start heading into town again?'

'For the time being you can relax. Our "sleeper" will let us know as soon as Franco or any of his outfit come back. Their idea is that if we aren't prepared for them, they can land a massive cargo of drugs, but we've got a shadow team of Police and Customs ready to go into action as soon as we're given the word that they've returned.'

'Well, I appreciate you coming to tell me. And I take it you're going to use up some of the leave you're owed?'

'That's my intention,' Latham said, 'although I'm never completely off-duty. I'm always keeping abreast of the drug situation.'

Baxter thought of what Lester had revealed about Latham's brother: a tragedy that obviously drove the detective on. Baxter had a lot of time for Ian Latham—he considered him an outstanding police officer who'd exhibited a willingness to work outside the official system. Latham would always have his co-operation.

'As much as I like you, Ian, I hope I don't see you again in a professional capacity,' Baxter said, smiling, before Latham headed out the door.

The detective shook his hand again. 'Stay loose, champ. I'll be in touch.'

●

Months passed while peace reigned over the river. Baxter was slogging away at his novel and was pleased with what he'd written. He went out fishing with Steve Lewis and spent time with the Lewises, and spoke to Liz and his mother on the phone.

And, of course, he saw Julie. There had been no perceptible change in her attitude—she still came out and fished with him, and he cooked her special meals.

One evening, Baxter received an unexpected phone call from Liz. There was something strange in her voice when she said hello. Then, without warning, she told him she'd had a baby boy. She sounded overjoyed.

'Is it mine?' Baxter asked, his heart racing.

'Of course! And I've named him after you.'

He wasn't sure what else to ask. 'Is he a good baby?'

'Fantastic. He weighed ten pounds.'

'That's pretty big. Any problems?'

'None beyond the usual, so I was told.'

Baxter was shell-shocked. Out of the blue, he was going to be a father. Of course, this didn't mean that he would marry Liz. He still felt warmly towards her—although he wished she'd told him about the baby a little earlier!—and he still didn't love her. But he did think of how pleased his mother would be. He simply wasn't sure how to tell her.

The next day, Julie dropped by and she seemed troubled. When he told her the news, he could see she already knew. In fact, it turned out, Liz had called her.

'Is it Greg's?' Julie had asked.

'Of course,' Liz had said.

'Does he know?'

'Not yet. I wanted you to be the first to know.'

'I would have thought Greg should be the first.'

'Oh, I'll tell him,' Liz had said. 'I've just been a wee bit scared of how he'll react.'

In Julie's opinion, Liz had derived no small amount of satisfaction from the situation. And for the first time, to his own satisfaction, Baxter was almost certain he heard jealousy in Julie's voice.

Because he was still coming to terms with the news, he asked her to keep it under her hat, and she readily agreed.

CHAPTER THIRTY-FOUR

Baxter had a meal with the Lewises about once a week, usually dinner. They'd often eat a new dish from him, although sometimes Jane would try her hand at something he'd cooked in the past. If it was a dish of any complexity, Julie gave a hand, and though at first disinterested in cooking, Sherrie had gradually become involved too.

Jason didn't cook, but he just about worshipped Baxter: all it took was a 'How are you doing, Tiger?' and Jason's face would light up. He lived in hope that Baxter would teach him martial arts, and Baxter had told Lewis he'd start doing this once the book was out of the way.

Meals with the Lewises were generally accompanied by robust discussions in which Sherrie, the school's champion debater, took a leading part. Very intelligent and with well-formed opinions, the girl could hold her own with almost any adult.

A few nights after Baxter and Julie learned the news from Liz, he and Chief walked into one of these discussions. This one just involved Julie, Jane and Sherrie—Steve Lewis was reading the paper and appeared disinterested in the subject.

Baxter had just sat down to some pre-dinner snacks when the words 'Liz Drew's son' caught his ears. He shot Julie a startled look and she gave him a reassuring smile—she hadn't spilled the beans. News of the boy's birth had somehow spread through town, although his paternity remained a mystery to everyone (not that there weren't rumours, of course). At Moondilla High that day, Sherrie and her friends had been chatting about whether it was right for a single woman to have a child.

'Why shouldn't she?' Sherrie said. 'If a woman can afford to rear a child from her own efforts and resources, why shouldn't she? Liz obviously has the money to bring up a child on her own.' The girl smiled shyly at Baxter. 'What do you think, Greg?'

'I think I'll have an orange juice,' he said diplomatically. He could see this discussion leading him into deep water—being the father of Liz's baby placed him in a very vulnerable position.

'So you're going to sit on the fence?' Sherrie said, surprised.

'You bet. What's doing, Steve?'

'It looks like being a dirty weekend,' Lewis said, over the top of the paper. 'No outside fishing for a few days. Your jetty might be the best spot.'

'How wonderful to be able to *abrogate*—' Sherrie sounded very proud of the word '—any discussion of an important contemporary social matter for fishing.'

'That's going a bit too far, Sherrie,' Jane counselled her.

'Greg is writing a lot about social justice and the like, so I'm sure he has an opinion about single mothers.'

Baxter realised there was no getting out of this one. 'I think it's mostly up to the woman and her circumstances,' he said.

'You don't need a husband or partner to have children these days,' Julie said. 'If women don't want a relationship but do want children, and have the means to look after them, they shouldn't be condemned for taking that route to motherhood.'

'Well, that's the approach of a radical feminist,' said Jane lightly. 'I happen to think that in the majority of cases, kids need a father.'

Julie frowned at her sister. 'It's true I want equality for women, but that doesn't mean I think dads aren't important. Our dad was great, and if I hadn't had him I would have missed a lot. I was never at odds with him like I was with Mum. That doesn't mean I don't support single mothers, of course.'

'Have you considered how a fatherless child would feel?' Jane asked, arching an eyebrow. Baxter had never heard her speak so heatedly before—he felt slightly worried about her reaction to him being the father in question.

'I should hope,' Julie said, fire in her eyes, 'that there'll be a more tolerant environment for a fatherless child to grow up in. It's happening now but is sure to be better in another ten to fifteen years. We will have moved on, Jane.'

'I think we have moved too far already,' Jane huffed. 'I don't fancy the idea of a child of mine going through life without its father.'

'It's happening,' Julie said. 'Look at Liz.'

Baxter cleared his throat. 'Well, if it were my child, I'd think about that child every day of my life, and visit as often as possible. A father can play a role without being in a relationship with the mother.'

'That's just how I imagine you would feel,' Julie said, smiling. 'I can't imagine anything less of you.'

'From what I've heard about men,' Sherrie put in, 'most of them wouldn't baulk at sleeping with a woman, whether it was for making a baby or otherwise.'

Jane shook her head at her daughter and smiled wryly. 'It seems to me that you're much better informed about a lot of things than I was at your age.'

'Yes, Sherrie has hit the nail on the head,' Julie said. Then a mischievous twinkle came into her eyes. 'Well Greg, seeing that we're all adults and discussing an adult subject, would *your* scruples be stronger than your sexual inclinations?'

'That isn't something I feel disposed to discuss here. I'm happier to stick to cooking and what Jane's going to dish up this evening.'

'Quite right, too, Greg,' Lewis said with a grin, folding up the paper.

'You men would stick together,' Sherrie said, scowling.

'I hope I've got the marinade right,' Jane said. She stood up and headed from the kitchen, releasing delicious smells when she opened the door. 'I put it in the fridge like you said, Greg.'

The joint opinion was that Jane *had* got the marinade right. 'To borrow a phrase, that was finger-lickin' good,' her husband said, and the others agreed.

'I must say you've added significantly to this household's culinary delights,' Jane said with a smile to Baxter.

He returned it. 'There's still my apple and rhubarb pie,' he said, and with a big grin Jason went to bring it in from the kitchen.

'Ooh, I don't think I should have any,' Sherrie said, pouting. 'I've cut out all cakes and pastry.'

'You don't have to eat the pastry,' her mother told her, 'and the apple and rhubarb won't hurt your figure.'

'Maybe just a small serving and not much cream,' Sherrie said as she eyed the pie.

Jason, who never gave a thought to his figure, expressed the common view of Baxter's pie-making ability. 'What a *yummy* pie. Who'd have thought you could make something so nice from stalks of rhubarb?'

'There's more than rhubarb to Greg's pie,' Jane said. 'There's apple . . . and then there's something else that he keeps to himself.'

Baxter smiled—she'd been pestering him for his secret.

'That doesn't matter, as long as he keeps making that kind of pie!' Jason said.

'Well, I must say that it's great to be able to enjoy another meal without worrying about Franco Campanelli and what he's going to do next,' Lewis said. 'I heard a rumour from a customer today that he's off in a Tuscan villa. Wherever he is, good riddance!'

He'd obviously intended it as a light-hearted comment, but the sudden mention of the drug smuggler's name cast a pall over the dinner party, as if a dark cloud lay across the room. Baxter had heard about the villa too, from Latham—but given other things the detective had been telling him, Baxter wasn't as optimistic as his mate about Campanelli staying there.

'What do you think makes people use drugs?' Sherrie asked, looking around at the adults. 'I've thought about that question a lot and can't find a single word that answers it.' Her eyes came to rest on Baxter. 'You must have done a lot of research about this, Greg. Why do you think people become drug users?'

He thought for a moment. 'As you've said, it's a complicated issue. If I had to make a stab at a generalisation, some people are dissatisfied with their lives, and the temptation is to make things tolerable with drugs. Prostitutes take drugs, but so do company directors. No matter how much money someone makes, or how famous or talented they are, they might not be satisfied with their lot and turn to drugs.'

'There's the peer pressure too,' Julie put in.

'Yes, very true,' said Baxter. 'A great many people think it's cool to take drugs, and that if you don't take them—at least try them—you aren't really with it.' He hoped Sherrie and Jason were paying attention. 'One thing I'm sure of is that there's no answer to be found in drugs. They give you a temporary charge, but the biggest charge is downhill. I don't know of anyone who's ended up a better person for taking them.'

'Well, it seems strange to me that so many people are prepared to spend so much money taking something that's bad for them,' said the ever-practical Lewis, who'd never had the slightest inclination to take drugs. Fishing was the only drug he needed.

'That's humans for you,' Baxter said, 'and there's always creatures like Franco Campanelli who profit from human weaknesses.'

'There's millions of dollars being wasted on that rubbish,' Jane said, disgustedly.

'And millions more being outlaid to try and stop it,' said her sister. 'But you can't turn back the clock. Drugs are here in town and I'm afraid they're here to stay, with or without Campanelli.'

'Oh, I don't know, Julie,' said Baxter. 'If he does come back and the police can do a job on the big bloke, maybe it will scare off anyone else who tries to step into his shoes—at least in Moondilla.'

Julie shook her head. 'How can that happen? Campanelli's

got big money behind him, he's got goons to protect him, and by all accounts he's got a police informer.'

'I'll admit he appears to be in a strong situation, but all of that can come crashing down overnight. One mistake could lead to a crack in his empire.'

'If so, I certainly hope it's not too long coming,' Julie said and sighed. 'This week I had two teenagers in surgery who were clearly drug-affected.'

'There's kids at school that are into drugs,' Sherrie said.

Jane's mouth fell open. 'Where do they get the money to buy them?' she asked.

'I don't know, Mum. I don't have anything to do with those kids.'

'Thank heavens for that!'

'Things were a lot better when fishing was the main interest here,' said Lewis. 'They were still talking about Zane Grey and his big fish when I was a boy. And couldn't that man write about catching them—hours and hours fighting swordfish! Then there was the thousand-pounds-plus tiger shark he caught off Sydney Heads. You ever read that stuff, Greg?'

'Not yet, unfortunately. I've been meaning to get hold of one of his books.'

'I'll lend you a couple. You can smell the sea in them and feel the lines going through your gloved hands. Blooming wonderful, they are. Nothing about rotten drugs.'

•

The news about the baby was pushed to the side somewhat by word from Ian Latham that Campanelli had returned to Moondilla. 'We'd always expected that he'd be back,' the detective told Baxter. 'This is his home, after all.'

CHAPTER THIRTY-FIVE

In the week since Campanelli's return, everything had been quiet. Then, very late one night, the phone trilled sharply in Baxter's office, where he was hard at work putting some finishing touches to *River of Dreams*.

'Damn the phone,' he said as he reluctantly reached for it.

Julie's voice was agitated. 'Greg, they've got Ian.'

'Who have and where?' he asked, his heart starting to pound.

'You know I often work into the wee small hours. Well, ever since Campanelli came back, I've been driving past his yacht on the way home. Sometimes I've pulled over and kept an eye on it for a while—'

'Julie!'

'I've been careful, Greg. And it was worth it. Tonight I saw Campanelli's thugs dragging a man up the jetty. I got out of my car and snuck a little closer—'

'Julie—'

'I'm sure no one saw me! But I saw it was definitely Ian. They must have woken up to him at last.'

'You didn't ring the police, did you?' Baxter asked, pulling on his jacket.

'No, of course not. I can't be sure I won't get Senior Sergeant Cross.'

'Good. But how many men are on the boat?'

'Four, with Campanelli himself. Apart from his two goons there's a fellow who's a kind of minder. He looks after the boat and does a lot of odd jobs.'

'Four men and they may be armed. I think we're outmatched, Julie. We might have to find a way to get the coppers involved—'

'There's no time for that! Look, I'm going with or without you. Right now they'll be knocking Ian about to get information. Then they'll dump him in the ocean.'

'They'll dump you too if you go meddling with them.'

'I can't stand idly by and let them kill Ian!'

Baxter knew she was right—he just didn't want her anywhere near danger. But he couldn't take on four men alone, and without the police, it was him and Julie together. *In that case*, he thought, *the more the merrier*.

'All right, I'm in,' he said. 'Ring Steve and get him to meet us near the jetty. He isn't a fighter, but he may be of some use.'

Julie agreed and named a particular side street as a good place to meet.

When Baxter put the phone down, he looked at the old shotgun beside his desk. He was tempted to bring it, but after a moment of thought he vetoed the idea. Instead he rammed a short ironwood stave in his belt. It was incredibly heavy for its length and as hard as iron, hence the name—a very handy weapon at close quarters.

He didn't even consider bringing Chief. The dog was loyal and trustworthy, but he wasn't trained for a situation like this. He was an innocent pet, not a police dog, and there was just too much risk of him being shot. Before Baxter rushed out of the house, he gave his mate a pat and told him to hold down the fort.

•

When Baxter arrived in the darkened side street near the jetty, he spotted Lewis and Julie waiting in her car. He parked and walked down to meet them, keeping to the shadows, then knocked on the window and got into the back seat.

Julie hadn't had to twist her brother-in-law's arm: when told that Baxter needed his help, he'd given Jane an excuse and left immediately. Julie had put him in the picture, so he was aware that they were almost certainly in for a scrap.

'How do we tackle it, Greg?' he asked.

'Head-on, Steve. There's no other way. The longer we leave it, the worse it will be for Latham. We'll have to put Campanelli and his men out of action. But Steve, I'm not expecting you to fight except in an absolute emergency. Julie, remember to go for vulnerable areas like the eyes and ears. And of course, if you get the chance, kick a man as hard as you can in the crotch—as many times as possible.'

She nodded and gave him a grim smile. 'I'm ready.'

'Let's go,' Baxter said urgently.

They ran up the jetty and then jumped across to the yacht moored alongside. A thick-set fellow wearing a peaked marine cap appeared at the top of the steps that led down into the yacht. 'Where do you think you fellows are going?' he growled. 'This yacht is private property. Clear off.'

'Mister, you've got three options,' Baxter said. 'One is to help us. The second is to leave this boat and walk away in one piece. The third is to fight us and cop what comes.'

The trawlerman picked up a fishing gaff and waved it in front of him. Baxter kept walking. As the fellow thrust the gaff at him, he caught it with his ironwood stave, twisted its head and pulled it free. He transferred the stave from his right to his left hand and hit the trawlerman a terrific blow on his jaw that dropped him to the deck.

'Steve, see if you can find some rope to tie this fellow up, then ring the police and tell them what's going on. Tell them to bring an ambulance. We're sure as blazes going to need one.' Steve nodded and got to work, and Baxter turned to Julie. 'If you're going to be in this scrap, stay behind me.'

He pitched the gaff overboard and ran down the steps, followed by Julie. At the bottom he smashed down the door of the yacht's saloon. Then he paused for a second.

Latham was hanging from a hook in the ceiling and two men were hitting him, one in front and one behind. The first man was big and ginger-haired—Skeeter, Baxter recognised, from the Family Hotel courtyard—and the other man had an Asiatic appearance, so Baxter guessed that he might be Yat Lee. Campanelli was sitting at a table that had been pushed to one side to allow the beating to proceed.

One of Latham's eyes was closed and blood was running from his nose. The sight of this good man being subjected to such treatment made fury surge through Baxter. His next movements were so swift that later Julie said she had difficulty recalling them.

Baxter jumped closer to Skeeter, then spun around, kicked up and caught the big ginger-haired man under his chin. The kick lifted Skeeter off the ground and broke his neck with a *crack*. He collapsed at Latham's feet. He'd been reaching for the pistol in his shoulder holster, but his hand had only closed on its butt.

'Yat!' Campanelli shouted. 'Get him!'

So this *was* Yat Lee. Lester's description of the man flashed through Baxter's mind: *If you meet up with him, don't give him any slack. He'd shoot or knife you and not think twice about it.*

The slim man came out fast from behind Latham with a knife in his hand. Its tip caught the top of Baxter's shoulder and blood began to run down his arm. Yat came at him again, but Baxter ducked then hit him across the arm with the ironwood stave.

Screeching in pain, Yat pressed his arm to his chest. His knife flew across the room towards Campanelli, who'd got to his feet to take a hand in the fight.

Julie moved to block him, then kicked upwards and caught him in the crotch. He grunted and reached down. Julie paused and, taking deliberate aim, repeated the sharp kick—twice. Campanelli swore and bent over, clutching himself, his eyes watering.

Meanwhile, Baxter smashed Yat and then hit him a terrific blow across the throat. Yat slumped to the ground.

Baxter lifted Latham from the hook, lowered him gently to the floor, then untied his hands and talked quietly to him. 'You'll be right now, Ian. The ambos will be here shortly and you'll be in hospital in no time.'

'Look out, Greg!' Julie screamed.

Campanelli had seized Yat's knife and was charging at Baxter.

CHAPTER THIRTY-SIX

Baxter pushed Latham to one side and side-stepped as Campanelli came towards him.

There was a report and then a second one. Campanelli stood still for a second or two and then crashed to the floor.

Latham, a police officer while he had breath in his body, dropped Skeeter's pistol, which he'd pulled from the shoulder holster. 'Only had one eye to see through,' he croaked. 'Did I get him, Greg?'

'You got him, Ian,' Baxter said, as the first of the police officers came through the door, followed by Steve Lewis. Baxter was relieved not to see Senior Sergeant Cross among them. Latham had collapsed across Skeeter's body.

'Christ, it looks like a war zone,' Lewis said.

'Let's hope it's the end of the war on drugs in Moondilla,' Baxter said. 'Where's the ambulance? Julie, what's the score with Latham?'

'It looks as if he's got a broken nose and I think he's concussed, but he'll need X-rays to check for internal damage. It's a miracle he had enough left in him to shoot Campanelli. Pure willpower. The ambos will look after him and I'll see him in hospital.' Then she took Baxter by his uninjured arm, her touch firm but gentle. 'I'll need to look at your cut before I go. You might need stitching up by the blood you're losing.'

'I got off lightly considering the odds.' He smiled at her, reaching up to take her hand. 'You distracted Campanelli long enough for me to deal with that creep.'

She returned his smile, her eyes bright and warm, and squeezed his hand.

'First you should make sure Latham's sorted out,' Baxter told her. 'I reckon I'll be here for a while if you come looking for me later.'

'Three men dead—yes, you'll be here for a while,' an officer said. 'Why didn't you let us know what was happening? It's not your job to tackle crooks.'

'You'd better ask Dr Rankin that question. Or better yet, Latham himself.'

'I've done all I can for him,' Julie said, getting up from looking at the prostrate detective. 'Steve, will you dash out to my car and bring me my bag? It's in the boot.' She handed

Lewis the car keys, then turned to Baxter. 'Off with your shirt, Greg.'

Yat's knife had almost sliced off a strip of skin on the point of Baxter's shoulder, and the wound was still bleeding profusely. 'I must be slowing up,' he said.

'If it was anyone else, they'd be dead. Nobody could be faster than you, Greg.' Julie eyed the wound. 'If I can stitch up that loose skin, you'll hardly have a scar.' Two ambos had placed Latham on a stretcher and were carrying him out of the saloon. They nodded to Julie before leaving. 'I'll get to the hospital as soon as I've finished with Greg here,' she told them.

Steve returned with her medical bag and she took out what she needed.

'This is the second time you've done a stitch job on me,' Baxter said, remembering their first meeting in Moondilla.

'I hope it's the last,' she said as she gave him a local anaesthetic.

Out of the corner of his eye, Baxter noticed Inspector Daniels enter the cabin. Daniels was the boss cop for the entire district—Baxter recognised him from the news but had never been introduced to him. He was a large man with a hooked nose.

'How did all this start, Dr Rankin?' the inspector asked.

Julie kept a thick compress on Baxter's shoulder while she waited for the local to take effect. She gave Daniels a short account of the assault on Campanelli and his hoods.

'Why didn't you ring us?' he demanded. 'This was strictly a police matter, not one for you or anyone else to get mixed up in.'

Julie wasn't about to be intimidated. She explained herself in a calm, clear voice.

'You aren't supposed to know that Cross is bent. Did Latham tell you?' Daniels asked sharply.

'Never mind who told me,' she replied, equally sharply. Then her tone gentled, 'Keep still, Greg. I'm about to begin stitching.'

The inspector gestured at the room. 'There's three men dead here. That's going to take a lot of explaining!'

'There would probably have been a dead police officer and a very good one before the night was over,' Julie said. 'As for it being "strictly a police matter", I should remind you that Campanelli twice tried to murder Greg by wiring his boat and then sending two of his hoods to kill him with iron bars. I should say it was anything but "strictly a police matter".' She took a breath, her fingers still sewing away. 'Even allowing for our rapid intervention, Ian has been badly knocked about. It's a miracle he was able to shoot Campanelli. But hopefully that's the end of the drug business in Moondilla.' Julie tied up the last stitch. 'There you are, Greg. You can put your shirt back on.'

Inspector Daniels was staring at her, his mouth slightly open.

'Any more questions for me?' she asked with a polite smile. 'I'm going to the Bega hospital now to check on Ian.'

'No more questions.' Daniels hunched into himself, defeated. 'I suppose you'll do the post-mortems?'

'I suppose I will,' Julie said brightly.

Baxter coughed to hide his grin.

'See you later, Greg,' she said. 'Don't do anything drastic with that shoulder and take a couple of aspirin when you get home.'

Baxter nodded. 'Tell Ian I'll see him when he's feeling better.'

As Julie left, Daniels transferred his attention to Steve Lewis, who'd been a silent bystander. 'Where do you fit into this? Another vigilante?'

'Not really, Inspector.' Lewis introduced himself and explained his role.

'Were you aware that Latham was an officer working undercover?' Daniels asked.

'Not until tonight,' Lewis said.

'Who told you?' Daniels was writing all of this down.

Lewis shot Baxter a glance, and he nodded a reassurance.

'Greg and Julie told me,' Lewis said.

'Christ,' said Daniels, shaking his head, 'no wonder Campanelli tumbled to Latham. The whole bloody world must have known his identity.'

'Not necessarily, Inspector,' Baxter put in. 'A cop might have let it slip to Sergeant Cross and he told Campanelli. And what about your man on the inside?'

Daniels stared at him. 'So you know about him too?'

'Yes. Latham felt he should fill me in.'

Daniels put a hand to his forehead. 'All right,' he said. 'I'll need full statements from both of you, about everything that happened tonight and everything you know.'

•

When they were finished, Daniels sighed and put away his notebook. He looked as though he needed a stiff drink.

'That's all very well,' he said, 'but there's going to be a lot of questions asked. Such as why a detective sergeant's rescue was pulled off by civilians, and why three men had to die in the process.' But then the inspector gave Baxter a half-smile. 'On the other hand, Ian can thank his lucky stars he had you on side.'

Baxter nodded—it was good to know Daniels appreciated his efforts, even if simply at a personal level. This seemed a good opportunity to ask an important question. 'What are you going to do about Senior Sergeant Cross?'

But the inspector immediately closed off again. 'That's a police matter and doesn't concern you, Mr Baxter.'

'You're surely not going to allow him to remain in the police force? There'll be an almighty scandal if nothing's done about him.'

Beside Baxter, Lewis was nodding firmly.

Daniels scowled. 'We'll attend to Cross, all right?'

'I hope you do. Bent police officers stick in my craw.' Baxter swayed with a wave of exhaustion and blood loss. He glanced at his watch and realised it was near dawn. 'If you've finished with us, we'll leave this lot to you.'

'We'll probably have to interview you formally,' Daniels said gruffly. 'We've got a mess here to clean up.'

Baxter had reached the end of his rope. 'Look, Inspector, as far as I'm concerned, you can take the credit for the whole caboose. Leave me and the others right out of it. You can say that, acting on information received, the police rescued Detective Sergeant Latham. In the ensuing struggle, three of the drug gang were killed.'

Daniels raised his eyebrows, considering this. 'I'd have to talk to the top brass.'

'Then talk to them. I won't contradict you.'

Lewis was glancing between them, looking a bit harried. 'I'd best get home to Jane and the kids,' he said. 'She'll be worried sick.'

Baxter nodded. 'And I've got a big dog who's probably missing me.'

'I'll be in touch,' Daniels called after them.

'Not too soon, I hope,' Baxter muttered as he and Lewis left the cabin.

The three dead men were still lying where they'd fallen. Baxter hoped they were the last drug smugglers he ever had to deal with.

CHAPTER THIRTY-SEVEN

Detective Sergeant Ian Latham was sitting up in his hospital bed when Baxter called to see him. Baxter had waited some days because Julie had told him that after two visits from the police, Latham needed a rest—the first visit had exhausted him, and she'd restricted the second to five minutes.

Latham's face was a mask of stitches and bandages. His nose had been reset and the cut over his right eye had been stitched. What could be seen of his face relaxed into a grin when Baxter appeared at his bedside and sat down.

'I've been wondering when you'd come,' Latham said.

'Julie kept me informed about you. You aren't a pretty sight. Somebody must have taken a dislike to you,' Baxter said, returning the detective's grin.

'It's what you can't see that's more worrying. I couldn't piss for days. Blood in the urine. Ever had a catheter stuck in your whatsit?'

Baxter shook his head and winced. 'Never had that pleasure. I hope everything's working again.'

'Yes, but looks like it's only temporary. They might have to operate again, because that big bugger kicked me and tore something.'

'He won't kick anyone else,' Baxter said.

'So I've been told.' Latham chuckled dryly. 'You did a job on those two creeps.'

'Well, you finished the job when you shot Campanelli.'

'Blooming miracle. Of course, you'd have probably nailed him, but I couldn't risk him getting to you with the knife.'

'You must have kept up your target shooting.'

'Even with one eye closed he presented as a pretty big target,' Lathan said with a laugh, 'and he was quite close up.'

Baxter laughed too, but it was hollow. He was remembering walking into that room and the anger he'd felt at seeing Latham tied up and tortured. 'So they were hammering you for information?' Baxter asked, and the detective nodded. 'How did they tumble to you?'

'Some cop let it slip to Cross about our man on the inside, so they tumbled to him first. He knew about me, but because he was in such a sensitive position, he didn't know much about the operation. They would've got everything they could from him, then sought me out.' Latham's eyes were sad. 'We're still hoping to find him alive, but it's doubtful. He's probably at the bottom of the ocean.'

There was a silence as both men contemplated this, and Baxter thought about how easily Latham could have met the same fate.

'There's some better news, though,' the detective said, brightening slightly. 'Cross is out of the picture—he shot himself yesterday. The police raided Campanelli's house and found a list of payments he'd made to Cross. That settled his hash.'

Baxter nodded, pleased. After his terse conversation with Inspector Daniels, he'd worried that Cross would never get his comeuppance.

'They found something else,' said Latham grimly. 'An underground room fitted out for kinky sex. Nice fellow, that Campanelli.'

'Like a snake's nice,' Baxter said, and Latham nodded.

Then he looked away and seemed slightly embarrassed. 'Thanks for what you did, Greg. It was a lucky day for me when I first called on you. My wife wants to kiss you.'

'Well, there's not much of *your* face she can kiss, Ian.'

They both laughed.

'You might not be pretty right now, but I hear you're an adornment to the police force,' Baxter said. 'A little bird tells me you made Inspector.'

'Yes, that's right,' Latham said and smiled. 'No more undercover jobs for me.'

Baxter didn't think he'd ever seen the detective look so happy.

'When you recover, be sure and bring your wife and kids to see me,' Baxter offered. 'I'll cook you something special.'

'Laura will like that, and I've got a young fellow who's dying to meet you. He wants to learn karate on the strength of what he's been told about you.'

'Good for him.'

Latham was looking quite worn out, and Baxter realised they'd been talking a while longer than Julie had recommended.

'Well,' he said, 'I'd better push off. I was told not to stay too long.'

'That sounds like Dr Rankin,' said Latham with a fond smile. 'She's been a tower of strength for me from the day I arrived.' He paused and gave Baxter an assessing look. 'But how are things with you and her?'

Baxter sighed. 'We aren't in a relationship, though I wish we were. I'd like to have kids and I'd like to have them with Julie. It gets me down some days, but I don't know what I can do to change her mind. I reckon she sees me as a brother.'

'That's a bugger.' Latham's eyes moved to look over Baxter's shoulder and then they widened a little. 'Speak of the devil,' he muttered under his breath.

Startled, Baxter turned to see Julie standing at the doorway. In her white lab coat and stethoscope, she looked every inch a top doctor. Baxter wondered if she'd overheard anything, but if she had she didn't let on. She calmly said hello as she walked into the room, then picked up Latham's chart and perused it.

'How do you feel today?' she asked.

'A lot better. It's a big relief to be without that catheter.'

'We'll give you another couple of days and then have a look inside you.'

'The sooner the better, Julie. I'm not used to so much bed rest,' he said gloomily. 'And I was hoping to be out of here in a week or two.'

'Well, I'm afraid to say it does seem you'll need a second operation to have a look at your kidneys. Better to get all the nasty stuff done in one fell swoop while you're here. You can have a good long rest after that.' She paused and half-smiled, giving both men a mysterious look. 'But you'll be relieved to hear that it's not all bad news.'

'Oh?' said Latham.

Her eyes gleamed with excitement. She glanced from Latham to Baxter and back to Latham, her professional mask slipping. 'I've just heard that a couple of the top brass will be coming to see you, Ian,' she announced, beaming down at her patient. 'You'll probably get some kind of commendation.'

'It's Greg here who should be getting the commendation,' Latham said, nodding to Baxter, who ducked his head in embarrassment.

'The only publicity I want is for my book,' he said. 'And if I deserve a commendation, so does Julie.'

She laughed delightedly. 'Thanks Greg.' She met his gaze and looked as though she wanted to tell him something important, but then her face closed off again. 'And now I must go. You're an important patient, Ian, but I do have others.'

'Be seeing you, *Doctor* Rankin,' Latham said. He essayed a big smile but the bandages made a mess of it.

'Keep smiling, *Inspector.*' She grinned. 'And see you, Greg. I'll keep you updated on the patient's status.' She took a final look at Latham's chart and left the room.

By what seemed mutual silent agreement, neither man brought her up again.

'I hear you're making a very generous gesture,' Latham said. 'Inspector Daniels told me that you don't want any public mention of your part in recovering me.'

'That's right. Much better that the police take all the credit. It's your job to tackle the drug pushers—and after all the time, effort and money you put in, you're entitled to reap what rewards are to be had from coups like the Campanelli business.'

'The media would make a hero of you if they knew the full story.'

'Then let's hope nobody leaks the full story. The fight against drugs goes on, but I hope I'm well and truly out of it.' Baxter smiled at Latham and got to his feet. 'Be seeing you, Ian—and don't forget about my invitation. I'm going home to have a fish. There's something remarkably calming about watching a line.'

'Be seeing you, champ.'

CHAPTER THIRTY-EIGHT

Now that the drug grubs had been dealt with, Baxter decided to take a trip up to Rockhampton to visit Liz and their son.

He mentioned his travel plans to his mother, but as he still hadn't told her about her grandchild, he gave her the half-truth that he was going to visit an old friend who'd moved to Queensland from Moondilla.

Frances's reaction surprised him. 'Would you like me to come with you?' she asked. 'I could share the driving and keep you company.'

'Could the restaurant get along okay for a week without you?' he asked.

'Quite. My assistant Henry could look after it very well and he enjoys being the boss cocky. Good experience for him.'

Good old Mum, Baxter thought. She was always there when needed. Well, she'd get her reward when they got to Liz Drew's property. He had been trying to work out how he could surprise her with the baby, and his mother had supplied the answer.

Baxter decided to bring Chief, who could sleep in the car and have his food packed in an Esky. Julie said she'd keep an eye on Riverview and water the vegetables and herbs, and the Lewis family volunteered to help out too, so that eased his mind.

He said to Julie that he'd keep in touch, but she told him to take a complete break from everything in Moondilla—he needed it. 'Try to forget about Campanelli and his sidekicks,' she said. 'Doctor's orders.'

•

Baxter drove north to Sydney, picked up his mother and set out for Rockhampton.

'If I was a magician, I'd turn you into my girlfriend and life would be just wonderful,' he said, as they zoomed up the highway. 'It would solve a lot of problems.'

His mother burst out laughing. 'For you, but maybe not for me! I like you as a son—I might not like you as my boyfriend.' She patted his hand. 'I wouldn't give up on Julie. Something tells me that she's about to make a big decision.'

'Really? What gives you that idea?' he asked.

'I rang her and she told me that she'll miss you, and that it would be the first week since you ran into her in Moondilla in which she won't be able to visit you. I call that *distinctly* promising.'

To Baxter this didn't sound all that significant, but he still felt warm at the thought of Julie missing him.

'About time too,' Frances added. 'She hasn't got all that many years left to have babies.'

He grimaced. 'Mum—'

'So, tell me more about this mysterious friend of yours in Rockhampton. A man or a woman?'

Baxter thought that the less said, the better. 'A woman. Liz Drew. She left Moondilla after her husband died. She owns a cattle property and has a baby. You never met her. She used to be with a country and western group. Very attractive woman.'

'Hmm,' said Frances. 'Another fish that got out of your net.'

•

Liz's property was well out in the bush, more than an hour's drive from Rockhampton. Her cattle were predominately Brahman or Brahman cross, and a point of interest for Baxter: after living in New South Wales it was a new experience to see so many cattle with pronounced humps. He'd been told that Brahmans had a high tolerance for ticks and weren't so much affected by heat as the British and European breeds—they would continue grazing when the other breeds looked for shade.

The homestead was massive, its verandahs so long that they seemed to merge into the horizon. There were at least a dozen outbuildings and the whole complex bore the appearance of a small village rather than a family home.

The heat hit mother and son as they stepped from the air-conditioned car. A cavernous shed with a yawning entrance promised some relief, so they got back in the car and drove into it. Frances was fanning her face with a magazine.

Baxter poured water from a canvas bag into a bowl and put it beside the car. 'Stay here, Chief,' he ordered the German Shepherd.

As he and his mother walked out into the blinding sunlight and heat, they almost collided with a young woman who had materialised from somewhere in the maze of buildings. She was a tall, slim woman in riding gear, and she carried a coiled red hide stockwhip in her right hand. Baxter reckoned that at a distance she'd almost pass for a young man—as Julie often did—with her slim figure and dark hair jammed under a white, very broad-brimmed Akubra.

'Can I help you?' she asked with a certain wariness in her voice. It was a softer voice than her appearance suggested it might be.

'I'm looking for Mrs Drew,' Baxter said.

'Liz is in town. She took the baby in for him to have another needle. She said if anyone turned up, she'd be as quick as she could manage it.'

'How is he?' Baxter asked.

'He's a bonzer baby.' The woman gave him a once-over. 'I know who you are: you're Greg Baxter, aren't you?'

'Am I?'

She smiled and shook his hand. 'I reckon there's probably not two men in the country who look like you. Liz told me all about you.'

'She did, eh.' He worried the woman might make a comment about the baby, but instead she turned to smile at Frances. 'This is my mother . . . Mrs Baxter.'

'Pleased to meet you, Mrs Baxter,' she said, and the women shook hands. 'I'm Pat. Pat Collins. I'm Liz's cousin. I managed the place while she was down south.'

Pat was probably in her late thirties. Her eyes were grey and there were tiny lines beneath them. Her figure was lean, like a length of whipcord. She had small high breasts that betrayed her otherwise boyish figure.

'Good to meet you, Pat,' said Baxter. 'You know, you're the first female ringer I've met. Although as a matter of fact, you're the first ringer I've met!' They all laughed and that made the atmosphere more amenable.

'There's more of us than there used to be,' Pat said. 'Women ringers, I mean. Mind you, a lot of the old diehard cattlemen wouldn't employ a woman to save their lives. Not them. But things are changing.'

'That's good to hear,' said Frances.

Pat gave her a smile. 'Well, Liz should be back for lunch as she left early. In the meantime, would you like a cuppa? I've got my own cottage.'

'A cup of tea would be great,' Baxter said, and his mother—who was almost wilting—agreed. 'But I've got my dog with me. All right if we get him?'

'That would be Chief, right? I've heard all about him too. Liz says he's some dog. Of course you can bring him. All our dogs are tied up right now.'

Pat walked back with them into the big shed and showed a lot of interest in the German Shepherd. Then Baxter, Chief and Frances followed the ringer across the square and around the corner of another big shed, which was partly filled with bales of hay.

Just beyond this shed was a neat cottage. The Baxters stood aside to allow Pat to mount the front steps, then followed her in. It was a three-bedroom place and larger than Baxter had imagined from the front view. A large horse yard lay perhaps fifty metres from the cottage. It was attached to a stable that, from what he could see, was divided in two. A nice bay horse was feeding from a trough in the yard.

'Been out looking things over,' the ringer said. 'Got away early.'

Baxter nodded. 'I take it you know a lot about cattle, Pat?'

'I reckon I know a fair bit. I was just about born on a cattle camp. Won my share of campdrafts too.'

'This would be a good place for a boy to grow up,' Baxter suggested, thinking of his son. 'He'd have his own pony and plenty of riding.'

'He'll have all that, but there's not much money in cattle right now. You need to have a connection with a food outlet or maybe have a small feedlot where you can finish cattle, except that these cattle don't lend themselves to that sort of thing. You need a fair splash of British breed in them if you're going to feed cattle. Liz is looking into it.'

Baxter nodded; he remembered Liz telling him about this enthusiastically before she left Moondilla. He hoped the reality of station ownership hadn't hit her too hard.

'Would you like a wash?' Pat asked.

'That would be great,' said Baxter. 'This heat is a bit tough on Mum.'

'Yes, I'm used to being in air-conditioned surroundings!' said Frances, fanning her flushed and sweat-beaded face.

After their wash, Pat handed them mugs of tea that were about three times the size of a normal cup and slabs of fruitcake large enough for at least two people. Frances did her best to eat and drink, then asked Pat if she could please have a lie down. The ringer set her up in one of the bedrooms.

'Liz has started talking about selling this place, on and off,' Pat told Baxter, sitting back down. 'But her old man loved it and would never have thought of selling up. He reckoned if he ever had grandkids, it would be just the shot for them. So I think it's partly sentiment that keeps Liz here. That and the hope that beef prices will improve. Then there's the young fella—if he takes after Liz's father, he'll be a fair dinkum bushie and want his own property.'

'Then perhaps keeping the property is the best plan for the future?' said Baxter. It sounded like a terrific life for his son.

'Well, Liz says if she sells up and invests the money, she'd be better off than she is now with all the worry of the place. But then she loves it here.'

'Does she ride much?'

'Oh, yes. Liz is no mug on a horse. She rode from when she could walk. She doesn't ride in drafts like me, but she's pretty keen on horses. So they're one reason she always decides against selling up.'

Baxter had other questions he wanted to ask, but reckoned it would be bad taste to pry and would also place the ringer in an invidious position. Liz would probably tell him all he wanted to know.

'It's a bit different here to Kings Cross,' he said with the memory of that place still clear in his mind after all the writing he'd been doing.

'I suppose so,' Pat said. 'I've never been there but I've read about it. You know the place well?'

'Well enough. I did some research there for a book.'

'Ah. It's a bad place for drugs, isn't it?'

'Bad enough,' he said—but then Moondilla had been too, until recently. He wondered what Pat the Ringer would make of Alan the Pimp or Campanelli the King Pin. She'd probably use her stockwhip on them.

'Bad women too?' she suggested.

Rosa's memory still haunted him. 'Not bad, Pat, just unfortunate.' He decided to change the subject. 'Is Liz well?'

'Fit as a fiddle. Looks well too. She fed the baby and all.' Pat grinned and her grey eyes softened. 'Liz thinks he's Christmas. Probably spoil him something terrible.'

'I hope not,' Baxter said quickly. He was still wondering if Pat knew he was the father, but he didn't want to ask—especially because Frances might overhear. 'Are you keen on country and western music?' he asked instead.

'I can take it or leave it,' Pat said with a laugh. 'Liz likes it a lot. She used to be in a country and western troupe.'

'So she told me. That's how she came to be in Moondilla.'

'What did you think of her husband?' Pat asked. 'I never met Jack.'

'Not much. He was an ex-pug and a boozer.' He wondered how much Pat knew about the marriage. 'It beats me why a woman who stood to inherit all this would marry a fellow like Jack Drew. Liz told me it was because she'd got sick of travelling all over the country, but it seems she didn't have to do that. She could have come home here.'

Shaking her head, Pat sighed. 'Liz was too proud to do that. She had a big row with her mother and left. She wouldn't come back while her mum was here. And then she lost her parents, one after the other.'

'Poor Liz.' Whenever he heard stories like this, Baxter felt immensely grateful for his own mother. 'So they never mended their fences?'

Pat's eyes were sad. 'No, unfortunately.' She got up and cleared away the dishes. 'You want to have a look around the property? I'll leave the homestead tour to Liz.'

'I'll let Mum rest a bit longer, and I don't want her out in the heat. We might wait until the sun goes down. How many acres is this place, anyway?'

'About a hundred and twenty thousand. Of course, that doesn't mean a lot in terms of what it can carry. You need a lot more acres to run a beast than down south.'

'It must take a bit of getting around,' Baxter said.

'That and all,' she said.

This seemed a strange expression, but then he remembered that many northerners often added the 'all' to their sentences. It set them apart.

'We've got bikes and a couple of four-wheelers,' Pat said, 'but you can't work cattle on them. They're okay if you just want to keep to the tracks and check out the watering points, but you can't use them for mustering in some of our country. You need horses there. You ride at all?'

'Afraid not. I was always too busy doing other things,' he said. He told Pat a little about himself—the writing, martial arts and cooking.

'Liz is busting to see you,' Pat said. 'She thinks you're the ant's pants.' Pat was looking out the window. 'She won't be long now. See that dust?'

The ringer pointed to where a long caterpillar of pinky-white dust was snaking its way through the olive-green scrub.

CHAPTER THIRTY-NINE

The Toyota Land Cruiser came to a stop beneath a massive eucalypt beside the homestead's wire fence. Baxter watched as the driver got out and walked to its offside. She looked up and waved to Pat Collins—and right at that moment Baxter, followed by his mother, walked out from behind the big shed into the bright sunlight. Chief was at his knee.

Liz ran full-tilt towards them. There was no swaying provocative walk in evidence now. 'Greg,' she cried as she fell on him, and then, 'Chief!', as she fell to her knees and hugged the dog. 'Lordy, it's good to see you.'

Baxter looked across to where the ringer had been standing, curious about her reaction, but she'd discreetly exited the scene.

'This is my Mum, Liz. Frances Baxter.'

'I know,' she said, a little nervously. 'I mean, I recognise you, of course. Greg thinks you're the world on wheels, Mrs Baxter.'

Frances smiled and gave her a big hug.

'Shouldn't you extricate the baby?' Baxter asked.

Liz leaned into the Land Cruiser to remove the boy from his seat. 'There, did you ever see anything like him?'

'Him' was thrust into Baxter's arms, where he immediately began to cry very loudly. 'Whoa, fella, I'm not going to eat you. Probably not used to a man, eh? Too many women around.' Despite the baby's tears, Baxter was pleased to see he was a handsome, hearty fellow. 'Well, he certainly looks healthy, Liz. Here, you take the scamp and I'll carry your bags in.'

They followed her into the monolithic homestead and were staggered by the dimensions of the rooms. Air flowed along breezeways from the verandahs that surrounded the building.

Then they entered a huge kitchen, with massive cupboards and a large walk-in pantry. 'There's a coolroom outside,' Liz explained. 'We keep veggies and other stuff in it. They'll keep for ages—saves going to town all the time. And of course, we have our own meat. You can put today's veggies there. I'll put his nibs down with a bottle and get these other things stored away, and then we can have lunch.'

'Is there anything more I can do?' Baxter asked.

'You could feed His Majesty his bottle, if you don't mind.'

Baxter looked across at her and smiled. There was less of the old provocative Liz now, and more of the practical station owner and mother. And she still looked great. She was wearing blue jeans and a cream silk blouse with a string tie, and her wide-brimmed hat was a pearl-coloured Akubra.

'I could feed him if that would help,' Frances suggested, holding out her arms.

'By all means,' Liz said. She handed over the baby and his bottle. 'He's inclined to drink it very fast, so you have to stop now and again.'

Watching his mother hold his son, Baxter grinned. He couldn't wait to see her face when she learned the truth.

'He's a gorgeous baby,' Frances said. She stroked his peach-fuzz cheek and smiled down at him as he started suckling the bottle.

'He's not bad,' Liz agreed. 'He's got nice-looking parents so he ought to turn out all right . . . looks-wise, anyway. There, that's that,' she said, putting away three bags of groceries. 'Will corned beef and salad do, Mrs Baxter? I'm not a fancy cook.'

'It will do just fine,' Frances said.

'Is he drinking?' Liz asked.

'Half the bottle has gone. He's a solid fellow. Must have been reared on a good paddock.'

'I breastfed him. I wanted to because I reckoned I might not get another chance.'

Frances nodded.

'He's not bad, is he?' Liz asked with obvious pride. 'What do you think of your first grandchild, Mrs Baxter?'

Shocked, Frances looked at her for affirmation.

'Yes, he's Greg's,' said Liz. 'He looks more like Greg than me.'

'Greg, *how* could you not tell me?' Frances asked, turning to her son.

'I didn't know until quite recently,' he said, just as Liz said, 'Greg didn't know until he was several weeks old.' They both laughed.

'Greg wanted to surprise you,' Liz explained. 'You fell into his trap when you offered to come up here with him.'

'Isn't he the schemer?'

'I learned from the best, Mum,' Baxter said with a laugh, remembering that he'd recently accused her of exactly the same thing. She narrowed her eyes at him.

'But how come,' she said, addressing Liz, 'I didn't get to meet you when I came down to Moondilla? You've had a baby together and I hardly know a thing about you. Greg certainly kept you quiet.'

Baxter wasn't sure how to explain their relationship to his mother, but Liz just smiled and said, 'We're good friends and we spent one night together.'

'Well, I never!' Frances laughed and cuddled the baby closer. 'When he's older you *must* come and stay with me, Liz. What did you call him?'

'Gregory James,' Liz said.

'This is *very* exciting.' Frances's eyes were shining. 'If I'd known, I'd have brought a bottle of champagne!'

'Oh, that's all right, I've got champagne,' said Liz. 'Greg won't drink it but we can, Mrs Baxter.'

'Frances! Please call me Frances.'

•

The women drank champagne while Baxter had his usual orange juice, and then they sat down to a wholesome lunch. Afterwards, the three of them settled Gregory James into his nursery for an afternoon nap. Frances headed to bed herself, pleading exhaustion from the heat, and Baxter sat drinking iced tea with Liz on the wide verandah.

'There's something I want to tell you about, Liz,' said Baxter. 'It concerns his Lordship in a roundabout sort of way.'

'What is it, Greg?'

'I want to tell you a story. It's about a girl who died not so long ago. Her name was Rosa Craig, and she was a prostitute. I knew her when I lived in Sydney.'

Liz laughed, disbelieving. 'Don't tell me you were with a prostitute?'

'Never. I did hold Rosa's hand, but that was when she was dying.' His voice roughened. 'She'd overdosed on heroin.'

'Oh, Greg.'

'It wasn't a very nice way for a nineteen-year-old to die, especially without a single member of her family at her bedside. There was only Mum and me in the room at St Vincent's Hospital.'

So Baxter told Liz about Rosa and Prue, about the Craig family in Albury, and about Alan the Pimp.

'What I came to understand,' he said, 'is just how important it is to show a child—whether young or a teenager like Rosa—how much you love him or her. I would hate to think that young Greg ever felt that he wasn't loved.'

'I couldn't love him more than I do,' Liz said passionately. 'He's practically my whole life.'

Baxter knew this was true, but he couldn't help being concerned. Not after everything he'd seen and learned. 'Soon enough our son will be a big lump of a teenager and much harder to handle. You won't have an easy task, whether you're raising him on your own or with a step-parent. Being a parent is a lot tougher proposition than it used to be. There are less jobs and more drugs, and affluence doesn't guarantee that kids won't be affected. It's parents that make the difference.'

'You don't need to worry. I'll never neglect our son.' Liz looked across at Baxter, and then got up and came to him. She sat on his lap and rested her face against his cheek. 'Rosa's death must have affected you a lot, honey,' she said softly.

'More than you could possibly imagine. But I had one thing in my favour . . . a great mother.'

'Well, I plan on being there for our son every day of his life, like your mum was for you—and hopefully he'll end up a lot like you.'

•

When they left the next afternoon, Liz was tearful and held Baxter close to her. 'Look after yourself, Greg. Bye Chief,' she said, and crouched down to hug the big dog.

'Say goodbye to Pat for us,' said Baxter. The ringer had shown them around the property a little at sunset and then had dinner with them, telling Baxter all about cattle farming. 'She appears to be a straight shooter.'

'I will,' Liz said. 'Pat likes you too—she's out looking at cattle or she'd be here.'

'You will come and see me, won't you, Liz?' Frances said, and hugged her. Baxter had left the two women alone that morning for a long chat, and he'd returned to find them as thick as thieves.

'I promise, Frances.'

'And if ever you need any help, no matter what it might be, you should come *straight* to me,' Frances added.

'Thank you. I can see why Greg is what he is.' Liz smiled at mother and son. 'Young Greg will have a super grandmother.'

•

They were well on the way, though still in the scrub, before Baxter spoke.

'Happy?' he asked.

'Happier than I expected to be. Liz is a fine woman. So how come you didn't introduce her to me in Moondilla?'

'I never considered her as a marriage partner. And I tried not to get too close to her because of Julie,' he admitted.

'You must have got very close to her to produce young Gregory James,' Frances observed.

'Close enough for that, yes, but not for more.' He glanced at his mother, afraid he'd see disappointment on her face. 'I suppose it isn't all that you wanted—Liz isn't family. But she does have my son. Half a loaf is better than no loaf at all.'

'I couldn't ever think of that lovely baby as half a loaf!'

'Well if there are no more, he'll have to do,' Baxter said.

'He'll definitely do, whether there are more or not,' Frances said firmly. 'He's very like you were at that age.'

'Beats me how you can remember. But if you're happy, I'm happy.'

CHAPTER FORTY

There hadn't been much time for Baxter to think with his mother beside him on the long trip to and from Rockhampton, and thinking was what he needed to do. There were aspects of his life that were far from satisfactory.

It wasn't that he was unhappy: he lived in a great location, he had his own boat and the fishing was very good; he owned a great dog, he'd nearly finished his first novel and he was developing a network of fair dinkum friends. Best of all, he believed that Mr Garland would have been proud of the work he'd done to help Moondilla. But what he didn't have was a wife or even a woman who could be described as a girlfriend.

Julie Rankin was unarguably a great friend. There was a degree of closeness between them that Baxter appreciated, but it was more like the closeness of brother and sister. It was a mateship that never expanded beyond a certain point, and he couldn't help finding this disappointing. The fact was, he knew now that no other woman would fit into his life as Julie would. He wanted to have children with her and for their family to be the rock to which he could attach his life.

They'd long since got over any awkwardness about being together, whether in his house or on his boat, and he knew that Julie trusted him never to touch her. Tough, because she was very touchable—there was never a day when he didn't want to touch her. But Julie seemed perfectly content with the status quo. It was a predicament to which he couldn't supply an answer. The answer had to come from Julie, and she was no closer to supplying it than when he'd arrived back in Moondilla.

The situation was made even more trying because his mother had so much time for Julie and wanted her to be his wife. Frances imagined that he wasn't trying hard enough to win Julie over, but he knew there wasn't anything more he could do. He'd partly got his mother off his back about her desire for grandchildren, but despite her words of support, he knew she wanted him to raise kids in a conventional relationship.

He was now fairly certain that Liz's one-night visit to him had been contrived partly in the hope that she would conceive a child. Julie hadn't told him this straight out, but had gone into some detail about a woman's peak period for conception, a subject with which he'd been totally unfamiliar. It wasn't a one-off discussion, because Julie often, even while they were fishing together, veered into medical matters.

Julie had a gift for making such matters easily understandable, which convinced him that she'd make a great lecturer. Baxter never found her boring. She was a very intelligent woman, and he loved her. He'd never said this outright, but then it seemed Julie didn't want to hear it: after all, she'd never displayed outright affection for him. She liked him as a mate and treated him as a mate and as someone she could relax with to a certain degree as a break away from medicine.

There was never a time when he could entirely forget that she was a doctor and surgeon. Baxter knew that some women around town called her 'uppity', or what passed for uppity—but people everywhere respected her. And she'd still sit with Baxter on his jetty or in his boat in old jeans and a man's shirt and talk fishing. She'd read his fishing magazines from cover to cover and could discuss every article in them.

Julie Rankin was, in almost every aspect, a jewel of a woman. It seemed, though, that she'd always hold Baxter at arm's length. He wondered if he could ever accept that this was the way things had to be.

•

Baxter had spent a night and a morning with his mother in Killara before leaving for Moondilla. He was looking forward to getting back to his writing and some fishing. And to seeing Julie.

He'd rung her from Sydney and told her when he'd be back, and she'd assured him that she'd watered everything and that the veggie garden hadn't suffered from any lack of attention. Vegetables and fruit rated very highly with Julie—she was always stressing their value in a diet. He told himself to be grateful for her caring friendship, and said to her that he hoped she'd come to visit him as soon as she was able.

Between him making stops for Chief and investigating various roadside stalls, it was getting on for evening when Baxter arrived at the Riverview gate. For some reason, the big outside light was on—he thought Julie or one of the Lewises must have forgotten to switch it off. But then he noticed that the yellow insect light on the front verandah had been replaced by a green light, and this puzzled him.

Chief, pleased to be home, was out of the car in a flash when Baxter pulled up beside the house. And there was Julie, waiting at the bottom of the verandah steps to greet man and dog.

'This is a nice surprise,' Baxter said as he got out of the car.

'What is?' she asked.

'You being here to greet me,' he said, smiling.

'Ah. I thought it would be much nicer to come home to an open house.' There was a strange expression in her eyes, one he didn't think he'd seen before. 'Weary?'

'Not too bad, but it was a long enough drive. Much better having Mum with me for most of the way there and back. She did some of the driving.'

'How did the Great Woman take to the baby?' Julie asked, as they walked into the house and Baxter set his haversack down by the door.

'Shocked at first,' he said, 'because he was the last thing she expected—but thrilled too. Over the moon, really. It's put a new interest in her life. She was very pally with Liz when we left. Mum says Gregory James is a lot like I was as a baby, which pleased Liz no end.'

'It would, knowing what she thinks of you,' Julie said, a little too brightly. 'Well, I've got some fillet steak for dinner because it won't take long to cook. We can have some veggies with it, and I found a rhubarb pie in your freezer.'

'Sounds good. I could eat a horse,' he said. They started preparing the food. 'Any problems while I was away? How's Ian?'

'Still recovering,' Julie said with a sigh. 'The latest news is that he may be invalided out of the police force.'

After he'd been promoted to Inspector! Baxter was stunned. 'What does he have to say about that?'

'As you can expect, he's not happy about the prospect. The force has been his life and he's totally committed to stopping drug pushers.' Baxter wondered if Julie knew about Latham's older brother. 'But I think he's done enough,' she said, 'and it's not that he wouldn't have something to occupy him—he's a very fine painter.'

'Is he really? I wondered about that. I'm not a great judge of art by any stretch, but it seemed to me that he wasn't putting much effort into his beachscapes.'

'I thought the same thing, but he's been painting in the hospital and one day he showed me a piece that surprised me. Streets ahead of anything else he'd done.'

'Maybe he was simply putting in time while he kept an eye on the drug mob?'

Julie nodded. 'I think he's good enough to hold an exhibition, and maybe he will if he's invalided out.'

'Ian is one of the better men I've known,' Baxter said.

'I'll second that.'

Baxter watched Julie as she moved about the kitchen. Something was puzzling him. Throughout the whole time he'd known her—even as a young woman—she had always been slightly aloof. Here, tonight, she was acting like a different person altogether. Gone was the superior air, replaced by a warm demeanour he'd never known in her. It was as if she was chatting to a husband or partner while preparing dinner and eating with him in her own home.

Moreover, when dinner was over, Julie exhibited no desire to leave. The washing-up done, she sat on a lounge and looked at him. He came to sit beside her.

'Something troubling you, Julie?' he asked.

She immediately seemed nervous, her eyes darting to the side. 'Why? Do I appear as if I'm troubled?'

'You appear a fair bit different to usual.'

'What's usual?' she asked.

'It's as if you don't want people to forget that you're a doctor ... a superior person. You were like that when you came to me as a young woman, and you've never changed. You've always stood apart from everyone else.'

She laughed softly. 'I'd suppose I can't argue the point with you on that score.'

'So what's going on tonight?' he asked.

'Well, while you were away . . . I've made some quite big decisions,' she said. Her hands were clasped tightly on her lap, and she still wasn't looking at him. 'Prompted partly by a conversation I had with Ian in the hospital.'

Baxter sat up straighter, remembering what he'd told Latham: *I'd like to have kids and I'd like to have them with Julie. It gets me down some days, but I don't know what I can do to change her mind.* Had his mate tried to meddle?

'Don't worry, Ian didn't betray any confidences,' said Julie. 'He just talked about how you're a remarkable fellow for wanting the police to take the credit for the Campanelli operation—that anyone else would have wanted to be a hero. And . . .'

'And?'

'I said it was in your nature—that you just wanted to focus on your book. I told him . . . I told him you were the best man I'd ever known, next to my late father. So then he asked when I was going to marry you!' Colour had crept into her cheeks.

Baxter waited for her to say more, but she fell silent. 'Well?' he prompted.

'I said I thought about it every day. I've come to realise that I'd like to have children and not be too old when I have them.'

There were tears in her voice, though not in her eyes. 'But I explained that I doubt I could be the woman you'd expect me to be as your wife. Medicine is so important to me and I couldn't give it up. I'm not like Liz—I could never stack up to her. I'd end up disappointing you.'

This was a revelation to Baxter. That Julie hadn't thought he would want *her*, the way she really was, had never occurred to him.

She kept speaking, her eyes cast down. 'Ian told me this didn't sound like something I should be telling him, but rather something I should talk to you about. That I wasn't being fair to you. And he was right. So I made the decision to have this talk.'

'I'm stunned.'

'Not *too* stunned, I hope. Look, Greg, the thing is, you've been a very distracting influence ever since I met you again here in Moondilla.'

He grinned. 'I have?'

'Yes, you have,' she said firmly, finally meeting his gaze.

'You could have fooled me,' he said, his grin widening.

'Do you think I'm made of marble? That I could fail to be affected by you?'

He sobered, not sure what to say, but he reckoned he should be honest. 'To tell you the absolute truth, I thought maybe you didn't have whatever it is that makes a girl or a woman want a man. Steve told me you never looked at a boy in school, and your sister says you've never had a male friend here, apart from me. Everything you said and did made me think you weren't interested in a relationship with me.'

'If I'd given you an inch I'd have been lost,' she confessed. 'I was so scared of letting you in and then being rejected. But the thing is, you've already become such an important part of my life. I missed you while you were in Queensland.' She took a shaky breath. 'I realise I haven't played fair with you, as Ian said. It should have been me who's had a baby with you. Greg, do you still want to be with me?'

'I'd marry you like a shot,' Baxter said quickly. 'You know I've wanted you ever since you first came to my classes, and I'd just about given up on girls after I lost Elaine. I gave up on you too, after you went to England. I couldn't believe my luck when I found you again here in Moondilla.'

'I don't claim I'd be an ideal wife—'

He shook his head at her. 'What's an "ideal wife"?'

Julie grinned, but then it faded. She seemed nervous again. 'I just mean I might not be up to much after a day's surgery, but I'll do my best in the . . . well, in the nooky department. I know that's an important part of any marriage.'

The thought of 'nooky' with Julie sent heat through Baxter. He recalled the secret Liz probably shouldn't have told him— that Julie had never been with a man. It made sense that she was worried about her ability to do the deed. He just hoped he'd have a chance to put those fears to rest.

'Whatever happens in that department is all right by me,' he said.

He wasn't sure if Julie fully believed him, but she nodded. 'There's one thing I can promise you,' she said. 'You won't have to worry about money. But if we have children together—and I certainly hope to—you'll have to take a fair bit of responsibility for looking after them while I'm at work.' She lowered her eyes again. 'You could get a lot more writing done with another woman. It just depends on how much you want me.'

Baxter gently tilted her chin so he could look right into her eyes. 'For a long time I've dreamt about you being my girl. Well, dreams sometimes do come true. I dreamt about this river too. Now it seems I've got you and the river.'

She smiled. And for the first time he'd ever seen, there were tears in her eyes.

Then she pulled away and stood up, and his heart clenched in disappointment.

'Are you going home now?' he asked.

'No.' Her smile turned wicked. 'I'm not going home tonight, Greg. That was another of the decisions I came to.'

He got to his feet and took her hand, lifting it and putting her palm against his cheek. She rested her head on his shoulder.

'Did you notice my green light outside?' she asked.

'Yes, what's that about?'

There was a note of mischief in her voice. 'You once told me that you wouldn't touch me unless I gave you the green light.'

'Then green means go, doesn't it?' he asked.

'It certainly does,' she said, and kissed him.

CHAPTER FORTY-ONE

Baxter woke up slowly. He became aware that he wasn't alone and that one of his hands was encircling a generous breast. When he opened his eyes, he saw Chief looking at him from beside the bed.

'Greg,' Julie murmured sleepily.

'Mmm,' he murmured back, as he pressed himself more tightly against her.

Then she wriggled away and turned to look at him, frowning. 'What a blow that I have to get up. I've got hospital rounds.'

'Hospital rounds will be a wee bit delayed this morning,' he said, wrapping his arms around her again. He pulled her close and kissed her.

'You'll be bad for my reputation,' she said with a laugh, but didn't try to escape.

'I'll be good for your reputation. People will think you're terribly busy.'

•

After a scrumptious omelette breakfast, Julie was ready to go back to being a doctor.

'Do you want me to come out for lunch?' she asked.

The significance of her question wasn't lost on Baxter, and he remembered the fears she'd expressed the night before—that she wouldn't 'stack up' against Liz Drew. He didn't want Julie to feel he needed sex around the clock.

'Don't throw your arrangements completely out of plumb,' he said. 'I'll be able to hold up until I see you tonight. That's *if* I'll be seeing you tonight.'

'Of course you will,' she said, kissing him quickly. 'What will you do today, Greg?'

'I'll have a fish and a think about my book. And a sleep— didn't get much of that last night!'

She laughed and kissed him again. 'You know, we'll need to announce our engagement at some point,' she said.

'How about next weekend, we'll go buy the ring? You have a think about what kind of a party you'd like.'

'Before that, I'll take you to see Mum. I suppose you realise you've never met my mother, in all the months you've been living here. She's not too happy about that!'

'I hope she approves of me.'

'Me too.' Julie sighed. 'She's a hard woman to please.'

'Well, I believe your sister likes me, and Steve's my best mate, so at least I'm assured of *some* family approval.'

Julie nodded and he took her in his arms. 'I'm truly sorry I kept you waiting so long, Greg,' she whispered between kisses.

'We'll have to make up for those lost years.'

'We made a good start last night and this morning,' she said with a smile. 'Well, I'd best make haste.' As she was going out the door, she gave Chief a pat and called out to Baxter, 'I'll expect fresh fish for dinner!'

He chuckled and called back, 'Yes, dear.'

He stood at the window, watching his fiancée's car drive down the track. He was on a high about the fact that he'd be seeing her again that night, but he still had mixed feelings about her departure—now that she'd committed herself to him, he wanted her with him for every minute of the day. He supposed he couldn't have everything.

'Well, Chief, we'd better go and see if we can catch a fish or two,' he said.

He was fortunate to have the river beside him. It was the avenue to the ocean and all it promised for the fisherman. Moreover, his lifelong dream of returning to the river had brought him Julie Rankin, and all she promised for the future. It was, in every sense, the 'river of dreams'.

EPILOGUE

Women's *Voice* staff reporter Jennifer Crompton recently interviewed author Greg Baxter, whose first novel *River of Dreams* burst onto the Australian literary scene with the impact of a runaway truck.

Greg is the son of Frances Baxter, who has made her own kind of impact as a chef extraordinaire and author of several bestselling culinary books. Greg himself is no mean hand in the kitchen thanks to a thorough grounding with the Great Woman.

He's also a martial arts guru—in fact, he's a very high degree black belt. As a teenager, he was a gymnast of near Olympic standard.

Our reporter says that a meal prepared for you by Greg Baxter comes as close to a heavenly experience as anything one could expect on this planet. There's only one snag, ladies: this hunk is married to a very lovely medico.

•

There's something mind-blowing about a wild river, especially the rivers of eastern Australia. When they're at their benevolent best they project a kind of paradisiacal ambiance without parallel elsewhere in Australia. When they flood, and they flood quite often, they swamp towns, drown farm animals and make a big mess of the countryside.

But if you've been very cluey, you can live almost alongside a river and not be affected by flooding. Old Harry Carpenter was one of these cluey people. Many years ago, he built the house where Greg and Julie Baxter live at their gorgeous property, Riverview, near the town of Moondilla in New South Wales. The river has never come near the house, so Greg and Julie have the best of all possible worlds: the river and all that it promises, and the peace of mind engendered by the knowledge that they'll never be flooded, no matter how high the water rises.

Rivers rate very highly with Greg. In his words, the Moondilla river fulfilled his innate yearning for peace and contentment, and provided the kind of atmosphere he needed for his writing. This sentiment might appear greatly at odds with his martial arts exploits—in fact, unless you're in the know, outwardly he's as mild-mannered a man as you would ever meet.

It was only through speaking to both police and some residents of Moondilla that I unearthed a very different Greg Baxter. And the deeper I dug, the greater grew my respect for the popular author. Baxter, so I was told, once killed two drug hoods with his hands and feet in self-defence, and put two others out of action for several months. He also saved one very good police officer from what promised to be a sticky end.

As the result of a tip-off, I managed to obtain an interview with a high-ranking drug squad detective, whose name I cannot reveal.

'What kind of man is Greg Baxter?' I asked.

'He's one of the most physically dangerous men in the country, or the world for that matter. Especially dangerous to drug pushers—he hates them. One on one, I doubt there's many men who could beat Greg. But for ninety-nine per cent of the time, he's just a great bloke. A really lovely man. It's the power he can generate in that one per cent that makes him so lethal. He's a wonderfully fit man and a colossal bloke to have on your side, but I wouldn't want to be up against him.'

So I went down to the South Coast to interview this 'lovely man', and I found him to be as kind and gracious as any man could be. While he isn't over the top about himself, he understands that some self-promotion is necessary to help sell his book, and he couldn't have been more co-operative.

JC: You've been described in some publications as a 'dropout'. Is this a description you'd go along with?

GB: It's true that I've dropped out of Sydney society. I became completely disenchanted with that lifestyle and with the way the city was evolving. There's a vast difference between the rich and poor, and there's the drugs. At the time I left Sydney to live in Moondilla, I'd been working as a journo, talking to homeless kids and teenage prostitutes hooked on heroin and cocaine. Eventually I'd had enough.

The turning point was listening to a nineteen-year-old girl talk about the number of men she had to have sex with to pay for her heroin. Her 'boyfriend' had got her started on drugs and prostitution, and he was taking money from her to pay for the drugs he was supplying her, in addition to a percentage of what she made. This grub was crooked on me interviewing one of his meal tickets, as he thought I was trying to wean her away from him. The girl was too far gone on drugs for that, but he didn't care about her welfare one little bit. He pulled a knife on me and I had to deal with him.

JC: You actually broke his arm?

GB: It should've been his neck.

JC: Is it true that you took that prostitute to lunch at your mother's restaurant?

GB: Absolutely. I thought the girl could do with a decent meal and I also thought, naively, that if she saw what was on the other side of the fence I might be able to persuade her to get treatment for her addiction. I'm pleased I took her to Mum's place because it was the last decent meal she ever had. To bring her into line, her pimp fellow wouldn't let her have any heroin. When she got some, she overdosed. She was taken to St Vincent's Hospital, and Mum and I were with her when she died.

JC: And this girl, or a girl just like her, was one of the central characters in your book?
GB: That's right. To a certain extent it's an obituary for her, and for all the other poor unfortunate women chained to prostitution by drug addiction.

JC: There's a lot of anger in *River of Dreams*. Are you a naturally angry person?
GB: Definitely not. You can't get to my level in martial arts without the ability to harness and discipline one's feelings, anger included. It's true that I'm angry: we're losing hundreds of young people to drugs and depression annually. That shouldn't happen. But I channel my anger into my writing, in the hope of making a difference.

JC: Can you tell me more about what makes you angry?
GB: There's a whole army of second-rate people who have stuffed up what should be the best and fairest country in the world. Brave men and women died to defend our way of life.

I knew and loved one of these men, a decorated World War One soldier named Albert Garland, when I lived in Moondilla as a boy.

Australia could have and should have set the standard for the rest of the world. Our country wasn't infested with religious fanatics and bigots like some others, and it had—and has— resources that most countries don't have in such abundance. There's also the fact that Australia has never been invaded, although it came close in 1942.

JC: Isn't it a fact that you're living a lifestyle that would be the envy of many people?
GB: I suppose so. I'm not earning much money, but I have a successful medico wife. Writing isn't an easy occupation, though. It's damned hard and solitary work.

JC: But you shouldn't be lonely now. You have a very lovely wife, and I hear that she exercises and fishes with you.
GB: I'm damned lucky. Julie is a woman in a million. Before her I had only my dog, Chief, although he's a dog in a million!

JC: Is it true that your wife first came to you to learn martial arts when she was studying medicine at Sydney Uni?
GB: That's true. She was a feminist and had done some outrageous things—I mean, outrageously daring things. Then she went to Britain to further her surgical studies.

JC: **How did that affect you?**

GB: I missed her. Of course she was a little younger than me, but we got on very well, although at the time she wasn't interested in men and had never had a boyfriend. I expected that she'd make a great name for herself as a surgeon and I was surprised to find that she'd come back to Moondilla. She came home to take over her father's medical practice when he died, and I met her when she stitched up my arm after an accident.

JC: **What kind of accident?**

GB: I had to help a couple who'd driven off the road and smashed their car.

JC: **I suppose Julie was just as surprised to find you here?**

GB: That she was. She used to come out and fish with me. She can tie two hooks to my one.

JC: **You're implacably anti-drug. Is this going to be a continual theme of your writing?**

GB: Certainly not, although it's an issue I do feel strongly about. I'm implacably anti-drug because we've created a society in which drugs are regarded by many people as an answer to their problems. They're not. Nobody forces you to take drugs, and there are plenty of things you can do instead, even if you're unemployed. You can do voluntary work for charities, both in Australia and elsewhere, and there's more satisfaction to be gained from involving yourself in that kind of work than in drugs.

I chose to write a novel centred around drugs because they represent one of the most significant problems facing modern society. What they're costing us, God alone knows, and it's all money down the drain.

JC: Will all your novels be concerned with social problems?
GB: I shouldn't think so. But anyone who has a conscience has to be concerned with social problems. They've been the basis for some of the best novels ever written. Take Dickens, Steinbeck, Cronin, and the best of our Australian writers. What did they write about? Social problems.

Not everyone is smart or has rich parents, and it makes me mad to hear the smart arses refer to others as 'losers'. We used to have virtual full employment, and I think the most important things a country can offer its citizens are a good education, a decent health system and a job. The fact that we can't offer everyone a job means that we've run off the rails and let our young people down. The decline in morality and the use of drugs are part of the unemployment syndrome.

JC: How would you rectify the situation?
GB: I think we need to introduce a form of National Service, at least for young people not in a job. Get them off drugs and teach them something useful, maybe incorporating a program of first aid. You can't have young people sitting about on their

hands or homeless. You need to give them a mountain to climb, even if it's not a very high mountain. Other countries have National Service but we seem to always rely on volunteers, except in the case of Vietnam which was a war we should never have become embroiled in. No politician would be courageous enough to broach the subject of National Service, of course, but I think it's what we need now.

•

There were more questions I wanted to ask, but it was time for Greg to do his daily martial arts and gymnastic routine, after which there would be lunch. I've never seen anything to approach Greg's athleticism or the controlled power he demonstrated for me. If Julie works out with Greg, as she assured me she does, it's no wonder that she's in such great shape.

'Phew' was all I could say when Greg finished. What more *is* there to say about a fellow who can smash timber and tiles with his bare hands? I'd wondered how he had been able to dispose of two tough crims, but after seeing him in action it was no longer difficult to believe he'd done it.

Lunch, Greg informed me, would be a simple affair. It may have been simple in his eyes, but it was one of the tastiest meals I've ever eaten. The centrepiece was a lamb roll encased in a clear jelly of rosemary and mint. There were small potatoes boiled in their jackets, eaten with either cream or butter, and a tossed salad with a mouth-watering dressing, the like of which I had never tasted before. A plate of cheese and biscuits was served last, with slices of watermelon and honeydew from the home garden.

We lingered over the lunch, maybe for a couple of hours, and then Greg asked if I'd like to take a short cruise on the river. I looked at Julie, who was in shorts and blouse, and said that I didn't have any suitable clothes for such an outing. Julie said that this wasn't a problem, as she could loan me a pair of her shorts. Now I have to tell you, readers, that there wasn't the remotest possibility that I would be able to fit into a pair of *her* shorts. I said I had a pair of jeans in my port and I'd wear them.

I've got to tell you that Julie Baxter in a pair of shorts and a plain blue cotton top still has more style than most women dressed in their best clobber. She isn't a young woman, but she's definitely all woman. Maybe it's the exercising she does with Greg, but when Julie walks she sort of flows.

What I found so refreshing and heart-warming was the way Greg and Julie work together. I never heard a cross word pass between them. While her husband was talking to me, Julie went ahead of us and slipped one mooring rope off the jetty, then sat down in the boat and started the engine while Greg took my hand and helped me on board. Chief, Greg's gorgeous German Shepherd, jumped into the boat and sat down next to Julie at the controls. Greg slipped the second mooring rope, and away we went. Julie looked after the boat while I talked to Greg. There hadn't been a word spoken between Greg and Julie, yet each seemed to know exactly what the other wanted.

So we tooled off down the river. Greg caught three flathead and tossed two of them back. Occasionally I caught the glances that passed between him and Julie, and I have to tell you that I would die for a man to look at me like *that*.

It was a magical afternoon with two great people. After a couple of hours leisurely mooching about on the river, we drifted slowly home. I had a shower and went out onto the front verandah to watch the evening traffic on the river.

Dinner was something else. The main course was a big snapper cooked in foil. Greg had stuffed it with tiny tomatoes and goodness knows what else: he wouldn't tell me. There was chilled white wine—which, Julie told me, they bring out for special occasions. Greg, of course, doesn't drink wine or any kind of alcohol, even expensive gifts from his famous mother, Frances.

The author came across as a man extremely fond of his mother to whom, he told me, he owes a great deal. 'Mum often disagreed with what I was doing, but she always supported me to the hilt. Mum is very keen for us to have children, and we both believe that children call for one's total commitment. That's not what a lot of children are receiving at home today, including some of those street girls I talked to.'

Julie put in, 'We decided we'd have a brief spell before we started a family, but it's taken longer than I expected. And it hasn't been for want of trying.' She laughed and shot a meaningful look at Greg.

'You're expecting?' I asked.

'Yes, I'm expecting at last,' she said. 'Greg is going to get the chance to be a real house husband because he'll be looking after the baby for some of the time. We'll have to try for another one or two because I'm not a young bird now.'

'You look good enough to be a young bird!' I said.

'That's Greg's exercises, but I'll have to cut out the more strenuous stuff.'

'You're going to carry on with the practice?' I asked.

'Oh, yes. The surgical stuff too. At least for a while.'

'And I suppose your pregnancy is a big talking point?'

'You could say that. Greg's mother is over the moon about it.'

'Does Greg allow you to do any cooking?' I essayed.

'Greg used to do virtually all of it, but I'm quite proficient now. I know I'll never be in his class, while he says he'll never be as good as his mother, but Frances disagrees. She's actually used some of Greg's recipes in her most recent book.'

I stayed with Greg and Julie that night, and the next morning Greg cooked the most mouth-watering omelette I've ever tasted. The man is a magician with food. Then the couple came out to the hire car to see me off. They stood together, hand in hand, as I drove away from that magical place with its lush shrubs, copious veggie garden and that long, lovely shining river.

I actually cried after they invited me to come again. I thought it was quite wonderful of Julie. I mean that if I had Greg Baxter, I wouldn't be keen to share him with anyone else. Not for about ten years, anyway.

Greg is certainly a very deceptive fellow. He's mild-mannered and softly spoken. If I hadn't seen him break those planks with his bare hands, maybe I wouldn't believe what I'd been told about him. Greg's exterior masks a man of great athleticism and lethal power. If I were a man, I wouldn't care to have him angry with me.

While Greg has a lot of anger in him, it doesn't show until he begins to talk about drugs, the decline in morality and unemployment. Greg talks passionately about these problems, and I believe that the anger he feels will be revealed in his books. And you can't help but agree that most of what he says is right. It's just that not many people write about these subjects quite so well or anything like as passionately.

So what was my most striking impression of Greg Baxter?

It would be easy to describe him as a great athlete, chef and author, but what touched me most was his obvious love for Julie and hers for him. It was there in a touch on an arm and a quick smile—small outward manifestations of regard for each other.

I'm surrounded by divorced men and women, so I have a somewhat jaundiced view of marriage. My mother, who has been married to my father for nearly forty years, says that many of today's people have no guts and walk away from marriage when things get tough. I cannot imagine either Greg or Julie walking away from a tough situation. I feel they would weather any storm and come up smiling. If ever two people were made for each other, they are Greg and Julie. It was a real privilege to visit with them, and I hope that when Greg writes more books I get the opportunity to interview him again.

Greg Baxter packs a massive punch, both physically and as a storyteller. And something tells me that he's going to make a great father.

P.S.

Dear Santa Claus,

I haven't asked for anything from you for many years, but please, please, can I have a Greg Baxter for my Christmas present? I promise I'll stop smoking and stop saying 'shit', and I will refrain from having lewd thoughts about my sister's boyfriend. I even promise to go on a diet, begin jogging and attend a gym. I'd like him for this Christmas, Santa.